S0-AKF-029

Noses Are Red

Richard Scrimger

BALWIN SCHOOL LIBRARY

Tundra Books

Copyright © 2002 by Richard Scrimger

Published in Canada by Tundra Books,
481 University Avenue, Toronto, Ontario M5G 2E9

Published in the United States by Tundra Books of Northern
New York, P.O. Box 1030, Plattsburgh, New York 12901

Library of Congress Control Number: 2002101142

All rights reserved. The use of any part of this publication
reproduced, transmitted in any form or by any means, electronic,
mechanical, photocopying, recording, or otherwise, or stored in a
retrieval system, without the prior written consent of the publisher –
or, in case of photocopying or other reprographic copying, a licence
from the Canadian Copyright Licensing Agency – is an infringement
of the copyright law.

National Library of Canada Cataloguing in Publication Data

Scrimger, Richard, 1957-
    Noses are red

ISBN 0-88776-610-2 (bound).—ISBN 0-88776-590-4 (pbk.)

    I. Title.

PS8587.C745N68 2002   JC813'.54   C2002-900774-7
PZ7

We acknowledge the support of the Canada Council for the Arts and
the Ontario Arts Council for our publishing program.

We acknowledge the financial support of the Government of Canada
through the Book Publishing Industry Development Program for our
publishing activities.

Design: Cindy Reichle

Printed and bound in Canada

1 2 3 4 5 6   07 06 05 04 03 02

To my parents

Acknowledgments

Many incidents in this book are based on real events. My own summers at Camp Pine Crest are green in my memory. I was, if I recall, a Chipmunk and a Loon, and you might say that I am still both these things. I would like – many years too late – to apologize to everyone else in the Lumberjack war canoe that capsized mysteriously in the middle of the big race. I lost my balance – what can I say?

And I would like to acknowledge my own poker friends. You guys taught me a lot about cards and people, and if you recognize yourselves or each other, you might be right.

On the work front, it is customary to thank agent, publisher, editor, publicist, and sales staff, and I am happy to do that (especially Sue, who said, "It's such a clean copy!"). On the home front, my wife, Bridget, was as supportive as ever. The name Zinta was chosen by my daughter.

You may find a number of words in the text unfamiliar. That's because I made them up.

1

Ahead of Myself

"Quick!" shouts Victor. "Quick, Alan, run for it!"

"What's going on?" I ask.

"They're everywhere! Hurry!"

He runs, pulling me after him by the neck. The dust cloud rises all around us, and the sound is in my ears – once heard, never forgotten – the buzz-saw whine of a million angry enemies. I can't get at them with the aluminum construction on my head. I run as fast as I can, considering that I can hardly see where I'm going.

"HELP! CHRISTOPHER!" I cry. "HELP, ANYONE!"

Wait. I'm getting ahead of myself.

Sorry. You're probably wondering what on earth is going on. *Who's Victor?* you ask. *Who's Christopher? What aluminum construction? Who are these angry enemies, and why can't you get at them?*

Fair enough. Let me go back a bit further, and start again. *Ahem.*

It all began on a beautiful spring morning about thirteen years ago. Cobourg, a pretty small town beside Lake Ontario – no, no, make that a *small, pretty town* beside Lake Ontario – was bathed in sunshine. The sky was a cloudless blue. The birds were singing their little heads off in the bushes outside the window of the hospital room. Inside that room was a tired new mom named Helen Dingwall. Mrs. Dingwall to you. She was learning how to put a cloth diaper on a baby. "Under and over," she muttered. "Around and up and pin it like . . . this. Oops!" She stabbed the baby with the pin. The baby opened his mouth wide and screamed.

"Oh, you poor thing!" my mom said to me. I screamed some more.

No, wait again. Come to think of it, that's probably too far back.

I'll try one more time. Fast-forward through my early years – teething, disposable diapers (finally no more pins!), singing "Clementine" to my nana while standing up in my crib, kindergarten, measles – and get to last June. I went to New York City to visit my dad. (My parents are divorced. No big deal. Maybe yours are too.) While I was having adventures with a snotty rich kid and her dog Sally (long story, no time to get into it now), my mom met Christopher.

He's important to this chapter of the Alan Dingwall chronicles, so I'll describe him right off. Christopher Leech: tall and thick, with thick dark hair and a thick dark mustache. Thick arms too – he's really strong. He can lift our big armchair over his head with one hand, holding on to the chair leg. He spends a lot of time lifting weights at the local YMCA – that's where he met my mom. He's kind of handsome, I guess. He has a lot of big sweaters. He's my mom's age, more or less. Old.

Shortly after I got back from New York, he moved in with us. He has a place of his own, but he stays with us for days on end. Sounds cosy, but it isn't really. There's something about him I don't like. Quite a few things, actually. His name suits him: Leech by name, and leech by nature. I don't like the way he dresses. I don't like the way he checks himself in the mirror. I don't like the way he peers around when he kisses Mom. He'll be giving her a peck on the cheek, and all the time his eyes are moving around the room, as if he's on the lookout for the cops. I wonder if he's on the run? It wouldn't surprise me.

To be honest, I don't like him kissing Mom at all.

We don't get on very well. He started off calling me my boy, and I told him I wasn't his boy. "I already have a dad," I said. "I'm *his* boy, not yours." Mom sighed, and Christopher apologized. Yesterday he tried calling me Young Dingwall. That didn't last long. "What are you up to tonight, Young Dingwall?" he asked.

3

"Playing cards, Old Leech," I replied.

He choked, spilling beer all over. "Why, you little . . . ," he began, and then caught himself.

In the evening Mom called me downstairs from the TV room. "Alan, I think we should have a talk," she said. I hate that phrase. I shuffled from foot to foot in our living room. We were all alone in the house; Christopher had gone back to his place to get some more sweaters.

"What about?"

"Sit down, first."

She patted the couch beside her. I took the yellow chair. I sat with my feet on the floor, then spun around so that I was sitting upside down with my feet dangling over my head.

"Alan, sit straight!" A harsh voice. You'd think she'd be nice, seeing as she works with troubled kids all the time, but that's the way it goes. I swung around so that my head was right way up.

"What should we talk about?" I asked.

"You and Christopher."

"Old Leech?" I smiled. I couldn't help it.

"Alan!"

"Sorry."

She folded her arms and spoke sternly. "I'm very worried about the way you and he don't get along. I'm disappointed in you, Alan. Christopher has tried to get along with you. He has done his part. He has extended the hand of friendship, and what have *you* done?"

4

Where does Mom get these phrases? Hand of friend-ship, indeed.

"I don't know," I said.

"You have slapped it aside. Christopher has gone out of his way to . . . Alan, look at me!"

I was staring out the window. I don't know about you, but when someone is yelling at me, I find it hard to stare deeply into their eyes and say *yes, yes, go on*. I turned back to Mom.

"Christopher has extended the olive branch to you," she said. "And you have . . ."

I didn't know what you did to an olive branch. "Eaten it?" I said.

"Alan!"

"What?"

"You have refused it. This situation must not go on. Don't you see, I care about you. So does Christopher. Both of us do. And that is why –"

"Here's Victor," I said. I was looking out the front window again. "He's early. The game doesn't start until 7:00."

"Game?"

"Sure. We're going to Nick's tonight."

"Cards again?"

"Uh-huh." I don't know why, but cards have really caught on this summer. We play all the time. Poker, mostly. Victor's dad found us an old carousel full of chips, and we carry it from basement to basement. I usually end up with most of the chips.

5

Victor Grunewald is my best friend. He's part of the story too. We've been in the same class since kindergarten. We looked like twins back then, but we don't now. He's grown up and out, and all I've grown is more red hair, and more freckles. I come up to his chin now, which isn't a great idea since he's beginning to get these pimples.

He's a nice guy, Victor. Very polite. He rang the doorbell and waited for me to come to get him, instead of just walking in, which is what I do at his house. He said hello to my mother.

She frowned at him. "I'm afraid that Alan won't be able to play cards with you tonight, Victor. We have some things to discuss."

He shot a look at me. I shrugged.

"Oh, sure, Mrs. Dingwall. I understand. Maybe tomorrow, or the next day."

She hesitated. "Actually, Victor, Alan is going to be busy for a few days."

"He is?"

"I am?"

Mom turned to me. "Yes, Alan, you are. Christopher is taking you on a canoe trip."

"Wow!" said Victor.

"*What?*" I said. I wasn't talking to Victor.

"You'll leave tomorrow morning, and be gone all weekend."

"Double wow!"

"*What?*" Still not talking to Victor. "But, Mom, I've never been on a canoe trip. I've never been in a canoe."

6

"Christopher loves canoeing. He knows all about it. That's why I suggested the trip. I think it would be a good way for you and Christopher to get to know each other better."

"But I don't want to –"

"Alan!" A warning note in her voice.

"You are one lucky guy, Alan."

"*You* can be quiet!" Now I was talking to Victor.

Just then Christopher pulled into the driveway, in his fresh-waxed cherry-red jeep with roll bar, extra chrome bumper, mudflaps, and fog lamps. Another thing I don't like about him. He swung himself out of the driver's seat and strolled up the driveway in hiking pants and boots, a camouflage shirt, and an Australian bush hat. Yikes. Joe Camping.

We all went outside together. Mom was pushing me from behind. "Hi, Mr. Leech," called Victor from the doorway.

"Yo, Vic!"

Yo.

"Hey, there," he said to me. Undecided about what to call me. "Ready to get wet and dirty, hey? Paddle hard, run hard?"

"Um," I said.

"Got a buddy flies a seaplane out of Rice Lake," he said. "Thought I'd ask him to take us to a conservation area north of Peterborough."

"Wow!" said Victor. "A seaplane. What kind?"

7

Christopher smiled at him. "Cessna single engine four seat."

Victor turned to me. "You'll have a great time!" he said.

"Uh-huh," I said.

All right, I was acting dumb and graceless. But I truly did not want to go camping with Old Leech. And, from the look on his face, I wondered if he really wanted to go camping with me. I know how strong Mom's *suggestions* can be.

"Gee, I sure wish I could go with you guys. I go to camp every summer. I love canoeing." Victor looked like he meant it. Actually, he always does mean what he says. It's what I like best about him.

"Sorry, Victor," Mom began, but Christopher and I interrupted together.

"Why don't you come with us, Vic!" The two of us stared at each other. Something we agreed on.

"Do you mean it?" Victor's eyes bulged. They looked like plums.

"You bet," I said.

"But, Christopher, honey, do you remember what we –"

"Hey, there, darlin'," he told her. I hate him calling her pet names. "It'll be okay." He put his arm around her shoulders and smiled widely. Big white teeth like piano keys. "What do *you* think?" *You*, meaning me.

"Great," I said.

"You see? He doesn't mind."

Mom didn't know what to say. Her idea was for me and Christopher to go out in the woods by ourselves and become best friends. Neither of us wanted to tell her that we didn't want to do this. And she didn't want to insist. An odd situation. None of us saying what we were thinking. None of us meaning what we said.

"Gosh, that's great!" Victor did mean it. "Let me ask my folks!"

"I'll come with you," I told him. "Bye, Mom. I'll be back in a while."

"Sure, Alan. Come along. My mom likes you," he said. And he meant that too.

2

Maladroitness

Victor's mom took a bit of convincing. "Oh, dear," she said. "I always worry when you go camping. What if you fall in a hole? Or get lost? What if you get hurt, little man, among all those lions and tigers and bears – then where would I be?" She talks with an accent something like the leprechaun in the cereal commercial.

"Aw, Ma," said Victor.

I giggled at the lions and tigers.

Victor's dad reached over to steal a gingersnap cookie. He doesn't worry about his son quite so much. "Vic'll be fine," he said. "And he can do with the exercise."

Mrs. Grunewald put her hands on her hips. "Exercise, is it? And what about you, then?"

"I don't need exercise. Why, I'm fighting fit. Look at that." He held out a muscular arm. Mr. Grunewald spends a lot of time shifting boxes and crates in his grocery store.

She laughed, and poked him in the belly. "Lard. All lard."

I swallowed the end of my cookie and reached for another one.

"Come on, Ma," said Victor.

She frowned.

His dad jerked his head at me. "You like those cookies, Alan?"

You can't go to Victor's house without eating. Most of your time is spent in the kitchen.

I nodded vigorously. "For sure. They're the best. Even better than the peanut butter ones we had last week."

Mrs. Grunewald softened. "An old family recipe. You'll take another."

"Thanks." I took a couple. She beamed down at me, a broad red-haired lady who looked natural in an apron.

"Please let Victor go camping, Mrs. Grunewald," I said. "We'll have fun, and . . . Victor will be company for me. I don't want to have to talk to Christopher all by myself."

"That'll be your mother's new man?" Mrs. Grunewald looked at me shrewdly. "I've seen him around town. A well set up fellow, I must say."

"*Hmph,*" said Mr. Grunewald.

"So can I go?" said Victor. "Please?"

Mrs. Grunewald raised her eyebrows at her husband. He nodded.

"Well . . . ," she said. "I'll have to talk to your mother first, of course."

I knew what that meant. "Thanks, Mrs. Grunewald," I said. "Thanks, Mr. Grunewald. Come on, Victor, let's get packing."

"My sleeping bag's in my room," said Victor. We ran upstairs together.

"Hey!" Mrs. Grunewald came to the hall and called up after us. "I haven't said yes, yet."

Rice Lake at 7:00 A.M. A deserted sandy beach. A playground. A litter of docks and small boats, floating in the reeds. A metal shack with BEWDLEY TOURS on it. Christopher was off to look for coffee and his pilot friend. I climbed down from his little red jeep, shivering. Not from cold. It was a sunny morning in August. Not that cold. I was shivering from fear.

"That's it?" I said, pointing. "That's the plane?"

"Could be," said Victor. "It's *a* plane."

It was tied up to the dock beside the shack. There was a teeny little breeze, making teeny little ripples in the lake. And these teeny little ripples were enough to make the plane bob up and down violently on its pontoons.

"But it's so small. It looks like a model. The only plane I've been on was much bigger. Why, this one is so small it floats!"

"Well," said Victor. "Better than having it sink."

"Thanks a lot."

He wasn't worried. He yawned wide enough to split his jaw, and stuck his hands in his pockets. He wore army shorts, with pockets all over the place. He even had a special hidden pocket with a hidden zipper. I knew it was there because he'd showed it to me. Took him five minutes to get the thing open. Inside was a safety pin with a shamrock on it – a lucky gift from Ireland. "Mom gave it to me," he said.

Christopher came back with a little bald bowling ball of a guy. The bowling ball was drinking coffee and eating a donut. He didn't look like a pilot. He looked like a next-door neighbor – the kind of guy who goes for lots of walks with his dog and doesn't pick up after it. He stuffed the rest of his donut into his mouth and shook hands. His name was Art. His palm was sticky. He kept chewing.

Art led us onto the dock. Between us, Victor and I carried the food pack, which didn't have any food yet, just pots and pans. Christopher carried the tent, bedding, and spare clothes in a pack, with a special forehead strap. When he put it on, he looked like a *coureur de bois* in last year's history textbook – a *coureur de bois* with a Styrofoam coffee cup in his hand.

Close up, the plane still looked like a model. Every time one of us moved, the plane moved. Christopher noticed the expression on my face.

"Scared, huh?"

I didn't reply.

"Are you scared, Alan?" Victor said.

The engine started up. I screamed. Christopher laughed. Very funny.

I'm not going to talk much about the plane trip. It was short, as the clock ticks, but long long l-o-n-g in my mind. I felt about thirty years older when we – well, we didn't land, but it doesn't sound right to say we *watered*. We skimmed over the tops of pine trees, touched down, and skidded for thirty very long seconds along the surface of a silver lake, while I got my breath back and tried to clear my blocked ears. What made it worse was that Victor seemed to be having a wonderful time.

"Isn't this great?" he said, punching me in the arm.

"Great," I said.

There wasn't a litter of boats and buildings on this lake. There wasn't much of anything. One log cabin, with a rack of canoes beside it, and a long rickety dock pointing out from the rocky shore like a finger. The moment our bags were on the dock, Art turned the plane around and took off again. The plane lurched clumsily into the air, like a little kid climbing the stairs one at a time. The silence after it left was very loud.

We carried our bags to the cabin without speaking. It was colder up here than back home. I shivered and wished I'd brought my jacket. All I was wearing was a T-shirt with a checked shirt overtop and baggy bathing shorts.

The log cabin was full of outdoor gear. The old guy behind the counter was happy to see us. He didn't move from his stool by the cash register, but he talked all the time we were in the store. Mostly about stuff that was supposed to scare us. "I have to charge you a deposit on the canoe, in case it never comes back. Some nasty rapids around here. That lady artist is staying near them. I keep expecting to hear that search and rescue have found her body."

Christopher bought a detailed map of the area, and a waterproof map case. "Where you planning to go?" asked the old guy. "You hear all kind of stories. Bears, quicksand, you name it. I were you, I'd head south. Don't want to frighten these two fine boys."

He winked at us.

Christopher bought some food. The food *sounded* normal enough: pork chops and steaks, mashed potatoes and strawberries and chocolate cake – but it was all in foil packages. "Weird, huh?" I said to Victor, holding up a bright red package of PORK CHOPS.

"It's freeze-dried," the old guy explained. "It don't go bad, and don't weigh hardly at all. What's that one you have there? Spaghetti and meatballs? That's a fine dinner, now. That one little bag should feed all of you – even you, youngster." He winked at Victor, who blushed. He's sensitive about his weight. "I know, I'm the same way. Can't never seem to get enough to eat. Why, I remember my mother saying to me once – I'd 'a been about ten or thereabouts – 'Son,' she said, 'don't you *ever* fill up?'"

"Why does it matter what it weighs?" I asked. "We're in a canoe, aren't we? Won't the boat carry all the weight?"

He cackled. "You'll see soon enough. There's a good-sized portage at the end of Hidden Lake here. Now, will there be anything else? Fishing rod? Plenty of fish around. One of the kids at Camp Omega caught a whopper last year. Made the newspaper."

Christopher put his credit card out on the counter.

The old guy cocked his head. "Okay," he said.

Funny things, canoes. If you stand up in them and lean out, even the littlest bit, they tip right over, and you fall in the water. Guess how I found this out? *Brrrr.* Hadn't started our trip, hadn't even packed the canoe, and we'd had our first accident. Victor laughed. Christopher looked pained.

The bottom of the canoe flashed in the sunlight. It was made of aluminum. Good thing, too – if it had been a birch-bark canoe, like the ones in our schoolbooks, I'd probably have put my foot through it. The water was up to my waist. "Sorry!" I called, dragging the canoe to shore. "Wouldn't it have been funny if I'd had the food pack," I went on. "Imagine all that freeze-dried stuff landing in the water and inflating all at once. *Boom!* Pork chops and spaghetti and steak blowing up like balloons!"

Victor shook his head. "The food is vacuum-packed, Alan. It wouldn't have expanded."

"Oh." I still thought it was funny.

Christopher lifted the canoe out of the water and flipped it. I stood shivering while he and Victor finished loading. I offered, but they said they didn't need my help right away. Christopher lashed the packs – food, bedding and spare clothes, and a smaller one with emergency supplies – to the thwarts of the canoe. "If we capsize *again*," he said, with a look at me, "the packs'll stay in the boat."

And then we were ready to go. Christopher held the canoe close to the dock. I climbed carefully into the middle, and positioned myself on a pack. You know, it was pretty comfortable. I put my feet up and leaned back. I was still a little chilly, but the sun was starting to warm me up. Maybe this canoe trip wouldn't be so bad. The sun shone. The water rippled. The canoe rocked gently, like a hammock. The wind in the nearby pine trees made a gentle sighing sound. I closed my eyes.

The sighing sound got louder. I looked up. Christopher was the one doing the sighing – not the pine trees. His shirtsleeves were rolled up over his powerful forearms. His camouflage pants were tucked into boots. His face was a stern mask.

"You look great, standing there," I said. "Very . . . woodsy."

He shook his head.

"What?" I said. I looked at Victor. "What's wrong?"

"What are you going to paddle with?" he said.

Oh.

I got out of the boat again.

3

Paddle!

"Stroke! Stroke! Stroke! Keep paddlin'."

Christopher's voice.

"Can I get a –"

"Paddle!" The word rang in my head. Christopher used it whenever I asked him anything. Can we stop for a snack? *Paddle!* A drink? *Paddle!* A rest? *Paddle!* I have to go to the bathroom. *Piddle! – I mean, Paddle!*

In a past life Christopher would have been an overseer with a whip. I would have been one of the galley slaves.

We were in the middle of the lake. Hidden Lake – ha! It wasn't hidden from me. It was all around me. And I couldn't wait to get out of it. It seemed to stretch on forever. The shore hung in the distance, like a painting.

I'd already learned a lot about canoeing. I knew what a thwart was, and how to sit forward on it, with one knee on the bottom of the canoe, to paddle. I knew how to hold the paddle, and how to take a stroke. I'd rocked the boat a few times, but I hadn't tipped it. On the whole, I thought I'd done all right.

I sat in the middle of the canoe, staring ahead at Victor's broad back. When his paddle came up, out of the water, I brought mine up. When his paddle came down, I brought mine down. Up . . . and down. Up . . . and down.

Good news: I was no longer cold. What with all the paddling, and the sun staying out, I was warm enough. Some parts of my body – the palms of my hands, for instance – were uncomfortably hot. I could feel blisters beginning to bulge.

Up . . . and down. Up . . . and – *splash!*

"Sorry!" I called over my shoulder to Christopher. Not the first time I'd splashed him. I'd splashed Victor too. I was like a fountain in the middle of the canoe.

"Paddle!"

Grrr.

And then the far shore, the oh-so-distant shore, which had stayed the same distance away for the longest time, began to move towards us. With every stroke of my paddle, it came closer.

The evergreen forest wrapped itself around the edge of the lake, a warm and unbroken line, except for one spot.

A splash of dark brown; a rip in the blanket of green. Christopher steered us towards it with powerful strokes. Nearer and nearer we came. I could smell the trees now. Peering carefully over the side of the canoe, I could see the rocky bottom of the lake, bending up to meet us.

Crunch. We touched. We'd made it.

"Stop paddling!"

Oh, right. "Sorry," I said.

Victor hopped out of the front and pulled us up the rocky beach. Now mine weren't the only wet running shoes. I stretched and stared back across the lake. "That was a nice trip," I said to Christopher.

He was busy unlashing the packs. I stretched some more. "Did you think it was going to take all day?" I asked. "It's only 10:15. We must be better paddlers than you thought."

He didn't answer. Head down, he was concentrating on the job at hand. When he freed a pack, he hurled it to the dry ground and moved on to the next one.

"What about you, Victor?" I climbed out of the canoe and went over to where my friend was busy collecting the packs and paddles into a pile. "Want a game of cards? I brought some." He didn't reply.

I shielded my eyes from the sun and looked around. "What's that diamond marker on the tree?" I asked.

"It marks the start of the portage," Victor replied.

"Oh. Where do you think it ends?"

"You've never been camping, have you, Alan? It ends

at the next lake. There'll be other markers as we go along the trail."

Gradually it dawned on me that the canoe trip was not over. We were not staying here. Not for the night, not for an hour. Christopher lifted the empty canoe out of the water and flipped it over and onto his shoulders in one smooth easy motion. He carried it over to us and stopped. What now?

"C'mere, you guys," he said, and lifted the canoe up over his head like a big fat barbell.

"Wow, are you strong!" Victor said.

Christopher smiled. He didn't even look like he was straining. "C'mere," he said.

We shuffled over and stood close together. Christopher lowered the canoe onto our shoulders. My first thought was: it's heavy. I bet birch-bark canoes were lighter.

It fit over us like the lid on a jar. Victor was at the front, staring ahead and down at the ground. I was at the back, staring at Victor's rear end.

"Next time I want to be at the front," I said. My voice echoed under the metal lid.

"C'mon, now," said Christopher's voice.

"Where?" I asked.

"Follow me," he said.

"I can't," I said. "I can't see anything except – that is, I can't see anything."

"This way, Alan," said Victor, leading the way forward. His voice echoed too. When he walked forward, the thwart bumped into the back of my head, pushing me forward. It was like being chained together.

"Fast as you can, guys!" called Christopher. "Along the trail. I'll meet you at the other end of the portage. Ha! Ha! Ha!" His voice trailed away, then came back a few seconds later. "Ho! Ho! Ho!"

"What's he doing?" I asked Victor.

"Picking up the packs," said Victor. "All of them. And the paddles."

My nose was itchy. I tried to scratch. Couldn't. Christopher's voice rose in one of those songs that army troops sing as they run along:

> We are strong and we are tough.
> Eat until we've had enough.
> Wear big boots upon our feet.
> Run so fast we can't be beat.

I may not have the words exactly right. You know the kind of thing I mean, though.

"Wow!" said Victor. "He's running up the hill with the packs on his back!"

> Sound off! Sound off!
> One two! One two!
> Three four! Three four!
> One two three four –
> Let's go!

Christopher's voice faded, away ahead of us. Victor and I followed more slowly. The ground was smooth at first, as we climbed up the hill away from the lake. Then the going got a bit rough. Victor almost fell, which meant that I almost fell too. "Sorry," he said.

"That's okay. Are we there yet?" I asked.

"No."

It felt funny to be following Victor, and asking him questions. He's bigger than me, and smarter in math, but he's shy. A bit of a scaredy cat, really. I had some trouble with bullies a year or so ago, and Victor was no help at all.

"Are we there yet?" My voice rang hollowly under the canoe. My breath, like a tennis player, came in short sweaty pants.

"No." Victor was starting to sound tired too.

"Are we going the right way? Can you see him?"

"Mr. Leech? No. He ran on ahead. But the portage is marked. We're all right. *Oops*. Careful."

"Careful of what – oh." A puddle right under my feet. Too late.

The path swung downhill. Victor stumbled forward, pulling me with him. I almost fell, for the eleventh or twelfth time.

"Careful!" I said.

"Careful yourself."

The path leveled out. I smelled water again. Stepped on a pebbly beach. "We're here!" said Victor. My first portage was over.

"What kept you guys?" called Christopher's voice. "Come on, now. Ho ho ho."

I had no idea how to get the canoe off my shoulders.

Fortunately, Victor did. "We'll lift together, okay?"

"Okay," I said. "Ready? One, two, three." I lifted. Nothing happened. I lifted harder. My arm muscles struggled against the deadweight. The canoe was as long as a car.

"Why aren't you lifting, Victor?"

"I was waiting for you to say go."

"Go!" I said.

The new lake looked a lot like the old one. Water on top, rocks underneath, pine woods wrapping the shoreline, hills in the distance. Now the sun was on our left, instead of in front of us. I could feel it on my cheek. I'd meant to pack some spare sunblock to carry around with me, but the deep pockets of my bathing shorts were as empty as my friend David's head – nothing there but gum. I took a piece, and offered one to Victor, in the front. He took it.

Christopher sat in the back again. The stern, I should say. His Joe Camping outfit was rumpled and wet. He took a deep breath of fresh air. "Paddle!" he barked.

Victor lifted his paddle and dug in. I copied him. Again. And again. And again.

Five minutes later, the shore behind us began to shrink away. Five lifetimes later, the shore at the other end of the lake began to creep closer. My jaws were sore from the gum. My nose was sore from the sun. My palms were killing me.

I stopped to check my hands. Yup. Blisters.

"Can we –"

"Paddle!"

I thought about splashing him, but I was too tired. Easier to follow Victor's stroke, and wait until we reached the end of the lake. The diamond-shaped portage marker shone like a beacon of hope. We'd have to stop paddling when we landed. Maybe Christopher would allow us a few minutes' rest. Ah, rest! Wonderful rest! We could get a drink . . . or a snack . . . or a –

"Paddle!"

Startled out of my daydream, I missed my stroke, and splashed Christopher.

4

A Cloud of Dust

Two lakes later it was coming up to noon, and I was ready to die. Victor was puffing pretty good too. Christopher was still singing his army songs, still paddling as strongly as ever. A machine.

This was a smaller lake than the others, but with the same water and rocks and pine trees. We hugged the shoreline. Up ahead I could see the portage marker clearly.

"Look!" said Victor, pointing with his paddle. "A loon."

I didn't know what he was pointing at. I thought loons were crazy people, so I was looking for someone on the shore going *blblblblblbl*, or hanging upside down in a tree.

Victor explained that loons are diving birds, but this one dove before I could spot it.

"Where do you think it'll pop back up?" I asked Victor.

"Paddle!" cried Christopher, the loon behind me.

Another scrunch onto another gravelly beach. "We'll stop for lunch at the end of this portage," said Christopher, wading ashore and gathering up the various packs. "You guys must be hungry."

"I'm okay," I said.

He raised an eyebrow. "Good. I put a bunch of health food bars in the emergency pack. I was going to offer you one now, but since you're not hungry, I won't."

"Alan!" whispered Victor.

"Race you to the end of the portage, boys. Maybe you'll be hungry then. Loser has to make lunch."

"Sure," I said loudly.

"Alan!" whispered Victor.

Christopher showed us the route on his map. The portage was marked in a dotted line. Straight ahead, then a small bend to the left, then a switchback and we'd be at the next lake. "Don't forget the switchback. It's a sharp turn to the right."

"Sure," I said. "No problem."

Victor and I had worked out a technique for lifting the canoe onto our shoulders without Christopher's help. We lifted one end off the ground, together, then he held that end while I crawled underneath the canoe, then I straightened slowly while he crawled underneath the other end. Christopher watched us for a moment, snorted, and ran off, singing:

You and Victor have to go
Even if you're kind of slow!
Crawl along the portage trail
Couldn't beat a slug or snail!
Sound off: One, two!
I will beat you!
Sound off: Three, four!
To the next shore!

His laughter faded into the distance. We set off after him. Victor in the front, as usual. A small rise, and then . . . down down down. Victor pulling; my neck taking a lot of the strain.

"Here's the bend to the left," he said.
"Are you sure?"
"I guess so. What do you think?"
"I don't know," I said. "I guess so too."
We turned left. Bushes and reeds all around us now. Not so hilly, and not so many trees. This trail was closer to the water level. What I mean is, it was swampier. The path was quite narrow, especially after the bend to the left, and when you stepped off the path you stepped into mud. The air smelled bad, and the hum of insects was all around us.
"Do you see the switchback?" I asked. "The sharp right turn?"
"No."
We squelched on. The trail was getting narrower and narrower. I could hardly keep on it.

"Do you think we already passed the switchback?" I asked.

"Don't know."

The trail wound around and around. Over rotten logs, beside stagnant water, through slippery mud. The forest closed in on us. The canoe brushed against overhanging branches. They made a loud noise against the metal.

"Are you sure we're going the right way?" I asked.

"No."

On and on. The canoe dug into my shoulders. I wondered if I was getting shorter, with all the weight pressing down on me.

"I hate mosquitoes," I said. Not that I was expecting a disagreement. Show me someone who likes mosquitoes and I'll show you an alien.

"Me too."

"Do you think he's finished the portage by now?" I asked.

"Mr. Leech? Yes." Victor stumbled, and stepped off the trail. The canoe bounced on my shoulders. Ouch. His socks were black with mud by now. So were mine.

And then he stopped. I nearly bumped my forehead on the thwart in front of me.

"Do you see the next lake?" I asked.

"No."

"What do you see?"

"Nothing."

"What?" I stuck my head out from under the side of the canoe and peered ahead at a muddy puddle surrounded by a clump of bushes and reeds. The narrow portage trail ran right to the puddle and stopped. Beyond the puddle was nothing except more bushes and reeds.

"This can't be right," I said. "Can it? Have you ever seen a portage look like this?"

"No."

"We must have missed the turnoff," I said.

"No, really?" Victor must be really upset. He's not usually sarcastic.

"Let's go back," I said.

There was no room to turn around on the narrow path. We'd have to go back the way we came. Fortunately a canoe has two front ends. "I'll lead the way," I said, spinning around under the canoe so that I pointed the other way.

Now, from under my outstretched arms, I could see a short way ahead. Better than looking at the back of Victor's pants. "Come on." I took off back down the path. "Look for a bend to the right," I said.

"You mean left," said Victor, from behind me. "Since we're coming the other way."

"Do I?" Victor's better in math than I am. "Well, you look for a bend to the left, and I'll look for one to the right. That way we'll have all our options covered."

Ten minutes later I stopped. "This is no good," I said. "I don't recognize anything."

"But it's the same trail," said Victor.

"Of course it's the same trail, but I was at the back of the canoe," I said. "For all I could actually *see*, we were walking past the Taj Mahal and the Eiffel Tower."

"*Hmm.*"

"You're at the back of the canoe. What can *you* see now?"

"The back of your legs."

"It was the same for me," I said. "What about turning the canoe around, so you go first? You'll be able to recognize things from a few minutes ago."

"Okay. Do you want to put down the canoe first?"

"No."

If we took it off, we'd never get it back on again. I didn't want to crawl around in the mud, trying to lift the canoe onto my shoulders. We backed up and shoved sideways, so that Victor's end of the canoe went into the bushes beside us. Then I pulled us forward into the bushes on my side of the trail. Then backward again, and then forward. We must have looked like a school bus making a U-turn. Finally we got all the way around.

Victor stuck out his head and took a long look up the trail. "I don't recognize anything either," he said.

"Oh."

He kicked the big rotten log at the side of the path. A cloud of dust flew out. Out . . . and out . . . and out. The cloud of dust grew before my eyes. And it made a noise as it grew, and billowed towards Victor. Some of the pieces of dust landed on his leg.

I wondered about Christopher. Was he worried about us? Maybe on his way to rescue us? Would it do any good to cry for help? I opened my mouth to say something when I heard Victor's scream, and felt the thwart of the canoe bang into the back of my neck, as Victor ran ahead.

3 0502 10024 1669

"What? What is it?" I was running too – I mean, I had no choice. Victor was pulling me. He was holding on to the canoe with one hand, and slapping at the dust with the other.

"Quick!" shouts Victor. "Quick, Alan, run for it!"

"What's going on?" I ask.

"They're everywhere! Hurry!"

He runs, pulling me after him by the neck. The dust cloud rises all around us, and the sound is in my ears – once heard, never forgotten – the buzz-saw whine of a million angry enemies. I can't get at them with the aluminum construction on my head. I run as fast as I can, considering that I can hardly see where I'm going.

"HELP! CHRISTOPHER!" I cry. "HELP, ANYONE!"

5

Things Can Always Get Worse

Running recklessly, charging through bushes and across little streams, racing as if we can't help ourselves, no time to spare for thinking about things like direction. My friend Victor, and me, and a boat the size of a Cadillac – stampeding because of dust.

Only, of course, it's not dust.

The bees are busy and angry. They buzz all around us. I'm terrified that they're going to sting me where I can't reach because my arms are holding up the canoe. I'm terrified that they're going to get down my shirtsleeve, or up my bathing shorts.

There's a clump of wings and striped bodies on the inside of the canoe, right – *right* – next to my hand. I jerk my hand away, and almost drop the canoe.

"Hey, watch it, Alan!" shouts Victor, running hard.

There's a buzzing noise right – *right* – in front of my face. I can't spare a hand to brush it away. I blow as hard as I can.

– *Hey, watch it, Dingwall!*

I shake my head. Hearing things.

My mouth is open. I'm breathing hard. Always tricky to breathe through your mouth in the woods. I've already swallowed a bunch of gnats and mosquitoes. But I can't close my mouth without cutting off my oxygen.

There's the buzzing again. *Right* at my nose. I can't see the insect – it's too close. I open my mouth to blow really hard, only at that moment I put my foot into a hole, and almost fall over. Instead of blowing out, I suck in.

In.

It's in my mouth. I can feel it. Oh, yuck!! And then – it's not in my mouth anymore. I don't actually swallow the insect. I know that. I can't feel it going down my throat. But it's not in my mouth anymore. It *was* in my mouth, and now it's gone. It didn't sting me. Did I spit it out? I spit again, just to make sure. The whole thing reminds me of the first time I met Norbert, last year.

Funny I should think of him. He used to call me by my last name – Dingwall.

I spit a couple more times, but nothing comes out – nothing except spit, that is.

Victor slows down. The bees seem to be gone. The buzzing has stopped. Amazingly, I wasn't stung once. "You okay?" I ask.

He nods his head. The canoe moves. "They were all around me," he says, "but they didn't sting me. How about you?"

"Same. I may have swallowed one, but I didn't get stung."

"Weird."

I have to ask a question. "Victor, do you have any idea – any idea at all – where we are?"

The canoe moves as he shakes his head.

We're walking through a swampy bit of woods. Reeds and scrubby trees all around. It's hot. The mud is fragrant and rich – like chocolate icing underfoot.

"So we're lost."

I'm not rubbing it in. I just want to know how badly off we are. And, in fact, we're pretty badly off. No food, no water, no shelter, no idea of where we are. No grown-ups to help us. We've got a boat, but no place to put it, and if we do find a place – a creek, let's say – then we'll be up that creek without a paddle.

Can things get worse?

Of course they can. Things can always get worse. I hear a rumble from inside my stomach, and realize that I'm starving. That's worse. And then Victor takes a step and disappears.

Worse.

I see the whole thing happen. I'm staring at him at the time. His foot – his left foot – lands in a puddle of black water and keeps going down. The puddle covers his shoe, and then his sock, and then his leg. Everything happens in slow motion, like in a horror movie. Soon Victor is up to his waist in mud, and going down. The front half of the canoe is still on his shoulders. As the boat slips forward, it pulls me down too. I struggle out from under the metal shell, landing on my hands and knees right next to the black water. *Whoa* – does it ever smell strong! I lever myself away from it, and climb carefully to my feet. By now the canoe is flat on the ground, and Victor has disappeared.

I'm still hungry, but I don't think about that now.

"Help!" That's me calling out. "Victor, are you there?" I bang on the canoe.

No answer.

Has he disappeared? Has the swamp swallowed him whole? Am I alone? That would be the worst thing of all. I scrabble around to the front end of the canoe, careful to keep to the dryer parts of the mud, and lever the front of the canoe up.

Victor's head is lying there. Like he's been – what d'you call it – decapitated. Staring eyes, wide-open mouth. Unmoving. His chin is resting on the mud. His head is the only part of him above ground.

Of course he's alive – his eyes flick left and right.

"Vic!" I say. He doesn't reply. He's too scared to talk. Too scared to move.

My hand is tired. I drop the canoe. Now he's gone.

I scrabble around and lift the canoe. There he is again.

It's scary, but it's also kind of . . . well, call me crazy, but it's also kind of funny. Reminds me of my grandmother's funeral. Everyone looking very solemn, Mom in a hat with a veil, and suddenly, all I could think about was a TV commercial where the world turned to chocolate. *Oh, Henry! Oh, Grandma!* says the kid. *What happened to you?* I laughed, and everyone turned to look at me with these mournful faces, which only made me laugh harder.

It's the same now. I know it's serious. I know that laughter is inappropriate ("Really, Alan, I'm ashamed of you! You're as bad as Uncle Emil! What would Grandma think?"), but I can't help it. It's funny. I mean, I'm absolutely lost in the middle of a swampy nowhere, with nothing but an overturned canoe . . . and underneath the canoe is a boy's head. I laugh and laugh, and Victor's head turns to stare at me, and his eyes get wider, and that only makes me laugh harder. I can't stop laughing now; it's like I'm riding a bicycle downhill, going faster and faster, and the brakes don't work. I'm too weak to stand up. I'm on my knees. *Everything* is funny. Victor opens his mouth and nothing comes out, and that's funny. I drop the canoe back over his head, and that's funny. I tilt up the canoe, and there's his head – *peekaboo!* – and that's so funny I drop the canoe again.

I'm hysterical. I want to stop laughing, but I can't, and there's no grown-up to take me to the back of the church. I'm gasping for breath. Tears are streaming down my face. My nose is tingling.

Actually, it's tingling in a familiar way. I stop laughing long enough to take a breath. I haven't felt that in a while. Not since. . . .

– *Good to know you haven't lost your sense of humor, Dingwall,* says a high squeaky voice.

"Norbert! You're back!"

– *And not a minute too soon. Look at this place. Dust everywhere! Who's been living here? Pigs?*

"No one's been there since you left," I tell him, scratching.

That was almost a year ago. I saw – no, make that *heard* – Norbert at the beginning of the summer, in New York City, but he hasn't lived with me since last fall, when I was having all that trouble with the bullies at my school. "Lived with" makes it sound like Norbert is in my spare bedroom. He's not.

He's in my nose.

I didn't realize until Norbert told me, but my nose is a big place. Your nose too. Bigger on the inside than the outside. In a way, it's bigger than you are. Apparently I have a living room, back room, bedroom, and kitchen (with appliances – Norbert loves to make cocoa in the microwave).

– *Mind you, it looks pretty good under the dust,* he says. *You've done some work on the living room, I can tell. And the garage renovation is new.*

"What renovation?" The garage would be for Norbert's spaceship. He's from Jupiter, you see. It may be the biggest planet in the solar system, but it has the smallest inhabitants.

– *Stop scratching!* he yells. *Anyone would think you were a dog.*

Smallest and rudest inhabitants.

"You should know about dogs," I tell him. He stayed in a dog's nose in New York. Sally, a lively and affectionate stray.

– *That was a mistake, and you know it.*

"Uh-huh." Would you believe I'm feeling better? Norbert hasn't done anything, yet, except insult me, but just knowing he's here makes me feel better. I'm not alone.

– *Honestly, Dingwall! You ask for help; I fly right over, and what thanks do I get?*

"That was you, then, just a minute ago? I thought I heard you call my name."

"Help! Help!" The voice comes from under the canoe.

"That's Victor," I say. "He's trapped down there."

– *I know.*

Victor doesn't understand about Norbert. He thinks it's me doing the talking in a high squeaky voice. "Don't worry, Victor, we'll get you out," I say. I lift the canoe off him. Now that I'm not laughing, I'm strong enough to move it away.

"We?"

"Norbert and me."

He doesn't say anything. His eyes travel up and down me. "You feeling okay, Alan?"

"Sure."

"You're talking kind of weird, like you did last year at school."

"Don't worry, Victor. Everything is going to be okay. Now, Norbert, what'll we do?"

Silence.

"Norbert? Come on, we're waiting for you. Tell us what to do."

Actually, I have no idea how we're going to get Victor out. I hope Norbert can come up with something fast.

– Say, when did you get the oil painting in the living room?

"Norbert?"

– I just noticed it. Very nice. The composition is very . . . plastic. There's something a lot like it in Frieda's father's office in New York. Impressionism, I think. Manet? Monet?

"Money?"

– Something like that.

"Norbert. Help us. What should we do with Victor?"

– Huh? Why, get him out of the mud, of course! And then wash him. He's very dirty, even for a human. You're not exactly a commercial for Time detergent yourself, Dingwall.

"*Time*'s a magazine. Do you mean Tide?"

– Whatever. And let's move it! Time and Tide wait for no one.

6

Chop Chop

I'm braced firmly on a patch of dryish land. I reach down. "Give me your hands, Victor," I say.

The sun beats down. The black rich-smelling ooze roils and heaves. Victor's hands appear above the surface, sprouting like flowers. I grab them and pull hard. He emerges slowly from the watery mud, gets a knee onto my patch of land and hangs there, panting.

"Come on, Victor."

"I can't." His voice is a sob. "My foot is stuck."

"Come on!" I don't know if I'm shouting at him, or me, or –

– *Look behind you, Grunewald!* shouts Norbert.

"What is it?" Victor tries to turn his head around. "What? What?"

– *On Jupiter we call them bears. Look at the teeth! Ooooh!*

"Bear?" Victor pulls so hard I almost fall into the ooze.

– *Here it comes!* says Norbert.

We pull desperately. With a sucking noise, and a sudden *pop*, Victor is kneeling in front of me. We scramble to our feet and start to run. Jump over a bush and run as fast as our muscles can move us. We run and run. I hear crashing behind me, feel hot breath on my back.

I'm not a fast runner, but I'm faster than Victor. I hear another crash behind me, and Victor's voice, cursing and crying.

– *The bear is going to get him*, says Norbert calmly.

"NOOOOO!" I grab hold of a tree trunk on the edge of the path, and turn around. I can't let Victor be mauled by a –

– *Too late*, says Norbert.

Victor is on the ground, his feet tangled in a patch of grass. He's sobbing, but he's fine. I run towards him. I don't see any bear. There's a bug on his arm. Victor swats at it.

– *There it is again! You killed it!* says Norbert.

"That was a horsefly," I say.

– *Did you see the teeth? Terrible.*

"Alan, what is going on?" Victor climbs to his feet. Mud dripping off him.

– *On Jupiter, we call them bears.*

"Why, Norbert?" I ask, but he doesn't reply.

"Hey, Alan, why are you talking in that squeaky voice? And what do you mean, on Jupiter?"

"Skip it," I say. He looks around.

"We should go back and get the canoe," he says. "If we can find it."

"Why?" I ask. I mean, what are we going to do with the canoe, once we get it? We've got nothing to move it around with, even if we had an idea of where to go. All we can do is carry it on our heads. A *moving* car is a wonderful thing – but if you take away the wheels, all a car is good for is keeping you out of the rain. It's a great big heavy umbrella. We don't need an umbrella now. The sky is blue, with a couple of playful puffy clouds.

Victor's peering back the way we came, trying to work out where the canoe would be.

"Why do you call them bears?" I ask Norbert. "Flies, I mean. They don't look anything like bears."

– *Because of what we have to do to them*, he says.

"Huh? What can you do to flies?" I say. "There's nothing you can do to flies. You have to put up with them, that's what."

– *Exactly.* He doesn't say anything else.

"I don't understand," I say.

"I get it. You can't do anything with them so you have to *bear* them," says Victor. I didn't know he was listening.

"Hey, that's good," I say. "I didn't see that."

"What do you mean? It's your idea. You made it up," says Victor.

I ask Victor if he has anything to eat. He shakes his head.

"I'm hungry too," he says. "Why didn't you take a health food bar from Mr. Leech?"

43

I don't want to go into that. "All those secret pockets in your pants," I say. "Didn't you pack *anything*?"

He checks carefully, and from the long and skinny secret pocket down his leg he withdraws . . . the safety pin, with the lucky shamrock on it.

I stare at it. Not much of a tool. "Remember that book we had to read in school, about the kid who survives in the wilderness with nothing but a hatchet. Remember?"

"What'd he have? A hatchet? Oh, yeah," says Victor. "He did everything with that hatchet of his. Yeah, I liked that book. What was it called, that book with the hatchet? Do you remember?"

I think hard. "Uh . . . wait a minute . . . *Alone in the Wilderness*? Or maybe, *Chop Chop*?"

"*Alone in the Wilderness*. Yeah, something like that. Not *Chop Chop* – that sounds like it'd be about a dinner."

"Yeah." I swallow, thinking about dinner. I bet the kid in the hatchet book would have starved to death if all he'd had was a safety pin.

"Hey!" Victor points overhead. "Hey, Alan! See that blaze?"

"No. What's a blaze?"

"That white mark on the tree. It's a trail marker. You know what, Alan? We're on the portage again."

"Great!" I say. "We're not lost."

"No."

"HEY! CHRISTOPHER!" I yell. "CHRISTOPHER!!!"
Nothing.

"Let's go to the end of the portage," I say. "Maybe he's waiting for us."

"What about the canoe?"

"We can come back for it. Let's find Leech first," I say.

We turn onto the path. We stay on the path. It climbs up a hill. So do we. We both keep shouting for Christopher. I am starting to get less hungry, possibly because I am starting to get seriously tired. I'm too tired to be hungry. It doesn't take long to get to the lake at the end of the portage. After only a few minutes, the trail swoops around a clump of pine trees and down a sloping rocky shelf to the edge of the lake.

Success? Not quite. Lots of sun, lots of rock, lots of lake, and a total lack of Christopher Leech. No packs, no note, nothing to indicate that he's ever been here. Which means either that we're in the wrong place, or that he never made it to the end of the portage.

What'll we do now? It might make sense to go back to the other end of the portage. Christopher would have gone back along the trail to look for us.

I don't want to go back. I don't want to move. "How about we stay here?" I say. "And wait for Leech."

"I don't know," says Victor. "What if this is the wrong place to be?"

"We followed the portage trail, didn't we? Blazes, and all that. This is the right place. Leech'll be along soon."

45

"I'm worried," Victor says. "What if he doesn't come? What if no one comes?"

I'm not worried. I'm too tired. I lean against a piece of rock. Nice soft rock. Makes a good pillow. I settle myself on my back, and yawn wide enough to swallow a football. "Then we'll die," I say.

He makes that noise with his tongue against his teeth. *Tsk tsk.*

I close my eyes. "Night, Victor."

I don't sleep for long because of the high-pitched whistling noise. It comes and goes, and comes again. A hissing noise. It's coming from near me.

"Norbert, are you snoring?" I ask.

No answer. The noise goes on. I turn myself over. The sound stops, then starts again.

"Alan. Alan!"

Victor's worried about something. I'm too tired to wonder what.

"Don't turn your head, Alan! Don't move a muscle!" he says. "There's a snake right beside you."

7

Owooooo!

I relax. I don't bother to open my eyes. I like snakes. I really cannot understand why so many people are afraid of them. Yes, they're long and thin. So what, so's string. So's spaghetti. So's my friend Henry, in school. I've never heard of anyone being petrified of spaghetti. There's the whistling sound again. Right near my ear. *Hiss.* Soothing sound.

"It's big," says Victor. "And it has these . . . patterns on it."

"Uh-huh," I say. "Don't worry. I'm tired."

The sun is hot. I lie flat out on the rock. I feel the energy flow out of me, like butter melting in the bottom of a pan.

"The snake seems . . . angry."

That'll be the hissing. Sounds like air leaking out of a soccer ball. "You're probably making too much noise, Victor. *Shhh.*"

"What if it's poisonous?"

"It isn't. This is Ontario, not Africa."

He keeps talking. "They told us about it at my camp," he goes on. "If you get bit by a venomous snake and you don't have a snakebite kit, you're supposed to sterilize a knife blade in a flame, and then cut two crosses over the snake's teeth marks and suck out the poison. Sounds gross, doesn't it! The farther away the bite is from your heart, the longer you have to live. If you were bit on the toe, for instance, you'd have hours and hours. What are you smiling at?"

"Nothing." I'm thinking of him cutting crosses in me with a safety pin.

– Hey, Dingwall, what's wrong with your heating system?

I'm too tired to talk to Norbert.

– It's getting hot in here. Where's the air-conditioning?

I'd tell him to shut up, but it wouldn't do any good. Telling Norbert not to talk is like telling the sun not to rise, or the peanut butter not to stick to the roof of your mouth.

– And what's with the shiver beside you? Sounds like a leaky hose. Last time I saw that pattern, it was on a pair of cowboy boots. Someone at one of k.d. lang's parties. He sang a song. I really liked it. I sang it in the shower for a while. Let's see if I can still remember it. Ahem. Ahem. . . .

"Alan, what are you doing? Why are you squeaking? The snake might get upset."

Not as upset as I am. "Shut up, Norbert!" I say, but I'm so tired the words lose their shape as they dribble out of my mouth.

> *I'm a lonesome cowpoke, breathing campfire*
> *   smoke,*
> *Nothing to live on but whiskey and beans.*
> *My stomach ain't healthy, my daddy ain't*
> *   wealthy,*
> *And I've got a hole in my new blue jeans.*
> *I'm feeling so strange, not at home on the*
> *   range.*
> *Owoooooo! Owoooooo! Owoooooo!*

It's ludicrous. I just want them to leave me alone. Does Norbert think he sounds like a coyote? He doesn't. More like a bagpipe, or like the music you hear from the guy sitting cross-legged in front of a basket, blowing into the –

"Hey!" whispers Victor. "Hey, Alan!"

That must be it. Norbert probably thinks he's being a snake charmer. I turn over and try to shut out the noise.

> *Yep, my cows lost their horns, and my spurs*
> *   are all rusted,*
> *Toes covered in corns, and my saddle is busted.*
> *My ten-gallon hat wouldn't hold half of that,*
> *And underneath it – I'm bald!*
> *My Colt 44 won't fire anymore*
> *And my dogies don't come when they're called!*

My pinto has mange, and I'm feeling so strange
'Cause I'm out – not at home – on the range!
Owooooooo!
Feeling downright strange, not at home on
the range.
Owoooooo! Owoooooo! Owoooooo!

The sound seems to go through my ears and right into my brain. I can feel the *Owoooooo!* vibrating inside my head. Really eerie. Reminds me of the alarm clock my mother got me a couple of birthdays ago. I hardly ever use it.

– *Owoooooo! Owoooooo!*

"Come on, Alan! Get up!" Someone is grabbing me by the shoulders. I try to open my eyes. My eyelids feel as if there are weights on them, pulling them down.

"Yes, Mom," I mutter.

"Alan! It's me, Victor! Stop singing and get up!"

– *Owoooooo!*

I get slowly to my feet. My head is ringing. It's hard to concentrate. I look down and – there's a snake all right. A big one. It's all coiled up with its head raised, ready to strike. What kind is it? Not a garter snake, with that oblong pattern on its back. The head sways back and forth as Norbert is singing.

Yes, I need me a change, I'm completely
deranged,
Nowhere near home on the range!
Owoooooooooooooooo!!

Norbert stops singing. The snake falls to the ground in a messy tangle. After a moment it unravels itself and pours away.

Victor stares after it. "That was pretty weird," he says.

I can't help but notice the rattle on the end of the snake's tail. The bite from a full-grown diamondback rattlesnake can kill you. This snake – as long as I am tall – was coiled beside me. I feel faint.

"What's the matter, Alan?"

"Huh? Nothing. Nothing at all."

The snake disappears into a hole in the rocks.

I clap Victor on the back. "Thanks, Vic," I say. "Thanks a lot."

– *Ahem. Ahem.*

"Oh, yes. Thank you too, Norbert."

8

Delta Winnebago

A chipmunk runs across the rock near my feet. A brown streak, on his way to his burrow under a dead tree. I stare, not the way I do at home, but with the added interest that comes from hunger. If worst comes to worst, we might have to eat chipmunks. I try to picture the little guy turning on a spit over a low fire. It's easy.

Of course, in order to eat the chipmunk, we're going to have to catch it. That'll be harder.

"What are we going to do about lunch?" I ask Victor.

"When I was at my summer camp, we learned how to live off the land. They taught us to make a soup out of birch-bark."

"I thought you made canoes out of birch-bark," I say.

– On Jupiter, I had a pet birch tree, says Norbert.

"What?"

– When it was hungry, it used to bark.

Victor is hunting through his pockets. "First we have to start a fire."

"With what?" I ask.

"With matches."

Of course he doesn't have any matches in his pockets. What he's got – all he's got – is –

"No way to start a fire with a safety pin, I guess?" I ask.

He shakes his head. "Maybe we won't be able to make birch-bark soup. You need fire to make fried moss too."

"You ate fried moss?"

"Uh-huh. It's full of vitamins."

"Good for it." I resolve never – *never* – to go to summer camp.

"We'd better forget about feeding ourselves, and look for Mr. Leech."

I don't want to walk anymore. "Maybe one of us should stay here, and --"

"No." Victor is firm on that point. "We stay together."

"But I'm so tired."

"He has the food pack with him."

Good point.

For the next hour we walk up and down the portage trail, calling Christopher's name until we're hoarse. About

53

halfway along, the trail splits in two. "This must be the switchback Mr. Leech was talking about," says Victor. "We missed it, coming the other way. We went down the wrong path when we were carrying the canoe."

On the far side of the switchback, the underbrush is beaten down. There's a blaze on a nearby tree. "This is where we came out," I say. "Somewhere back there is the canoe."

"Look here!" Victor goes down on his knees to examine a bright yellow scrap of paper, lying near the trail. "It's a health bar wrapper on top of one of our muddy footprints."

Health bar. The very mention of it brings water to my mouth. Oatmeal and nuts and raisins, maybe bits of chocolate or marshmallow.

"A wrapper," I say. "Is there any health bar inside it?"

"On *top* of our footprints," he repeats. "It fell after we were here."

"Let me see," I say. "Are you sure there isn't any health bar inside?"

"Someone was here not too long ago."

I check the wrapper. Check the ground. "Those aren't our footprints," I say. "They're way too big." I put my foot inside one of the prints.

"Must be Mr. Leech's then," says Victor. "There are health bars in our emergency pack."

"I don't know." I mean, the footprints are huge. Bigfoot, maybe. Or someone in snowshoes.

"Whoever he is, he may have more health bars," says Victor.

"Let's look around," I say.

"We have to be careful not to lose our way back to the portage trail," says Victor.

I'm not worried about getting lost. We left quite a track, last time we came through. A highway of broken branches. We search carefully, but don't find anything except trees.

What is going on? Where's Bigfoot? Where's Christopher? Where's the canoe? Hard to hide a canoe.

Victor circles wider and wider. No canoe. No Christopher. I call. No answer.

And then, under a bush off to the left, I spot it. Not the canoe – another yellow wrapper. With a health bar inside it. I pounce on it with a cry of triumph. I hold it aloft. I rip it open.

"Hey!" says Victor.

I divide the bar in two. He complains that my half is bigger than his half. How can that be? Halves are equal. My bite – and that's all it is – tastes more wonderful than anything I have ever eaten in my life. I lick the inside of the wrapper. That tastes pretty good too.

Victor moves further to the left. He's on his knees, reaching for something. "What's that?" I cry. "Hey, share it!"

He's found another health bar. "*I'll* divide this one," he says. You won't believe this. His half is *way* bigger than mine. I complain. "Fair's fair," he says.

My bite of health bar is gone. I look around for more. "Careful!" calls Victor, with a full mouth. I peer around.

Wait a bit. What is that yellow flash, away ahead in the bushes? I push forward. "Hey, Alan. Watch where you're going. I can't see you!"

Is it? Is it? Is it?

Yes, it is. Another health bar, peeking shyly from underneath a bush. The bars must have dropped out of the emergency pack as Christopher went this way. I grab it and pull the wrapper open with my teeth.

"Alan! Alan? Alan, where are you?"

I have the wrapper off the health food bar. I lick my lips.

– *Yoo-hoo! We're over here!* calls Norbert.

"Hey!" I whisper. "*Shhh.*"

– *We've found another health bar! Would you like some?*

"Shut up, Norbert!"

– *I thought we were sharing them. On Jupiter, we always share.*

Victor comes crashing through the bush. "Give me some!" he cries. He chews with wild eyes – well, he doesn't of course; he chews with his teeth, but his eyes are wild. He stares all around, and then bounds away into the bush. "Ha-ha! Another health bar – no, no, two bars!"

"I get one!" I say, bounding after him.

A whole bar to myself. I savor the entire experience. I feel life flowing through my veins. What an invention the bar is. How can I properly express my feelings towards it? I decide that if I ever become a rock star, I will change my name from Alan to Health Bar. Health Bar Dingwall. It has a ring to it.

– You know, this reminds me of a story I read once, says Norbert. *Two children lost in a wood, following a trail of food. What was it called now? Heckle and Jeckle?*

"Quiet, Norbert," I say.

– No, not Heckle and Jeckle. Davy and Goliath? No. Hatchet?

"Quiet, Alan," says Victor.

We forge ahead through the bush, Victor and I, shoulder to shoulder, eyes searching the ground for any more telltale yellow wrappers.

He sniffs the air. "Smoke," he says. I smell it too. I shout for Christopher. No answer.

The next two wrappers we find don't have any health bars inside them. *So* disappointing. Anticipation turns to resentment. Sometimes hope is harder than no hope.

Whoever opened the health bars was even hungrier than we are. The wrappers are in shreds. The ground is getting hilly. Rock underneath a layer of dead leaves and dirt. The slope is up to the left, or down to the right. We go right. Easier to walk downhill.

Victor's ahead of me. He throws up his hand dramatically. I stop. "Listen!" he whispers. I hear a rustling. "Could be dangerous."

"Could be Leech," I say.

Victor puts his finger to his lips. Then he points ahead, and makes a walking gesture with his fingers. Then he gets down on his hands and knees. Who does he think he is, a commando?

I give him the thumbs-up gesture. "Roger that," I whisper, as loud as I can. "Delta Winnebago Enchilada out!"

"*Shhh.*"

We creep forward. Victor stops behind a thick bush, and parts some of the lower branches to peer through it. This GI Joe side of him is unexpected. I peer around the bush.

In a small clearing sits a baby black bear. Cute little thing, with that earnest expression you see on young children who are concentrating really hard. Think of a kindergarten kid tying her shoes. In this case, the bear is opening a health bar.

Mystery solved. Well, one mystery. I know who – apart from us – is eating them. I still don't know who's leaving them behind, or why. I stand up, start across the clearing.

Victor pulls me back. "Stay away!" he whispers. "That bear's dangerous!"

What's he getting at? The thing is the size of a hamster. All right, not quite that small. What I'm getting at is that it is not a fearsome spectacle. It comes towards us, holding the health bar in its mouth. I go down on one knee and hold out my hand, the way you do to a kitten. "Hey, there, little guy," I say.

"Alan! Stop!"

"What?"

"Do you have a death wish? Get away from that cub!"

"Why?" The bear is rubbing its head against my hand. I like it. I've never had a pet, except for a turtle when I was small. It crawled under the sofa and died.

"Don't you know anything, Alan? Bear cubs are always near their moms," he says. "Moms who hate people messing with their cubs. Moms who weigh as much as a car, who have claws as long and as sharp as steak knives."

"Steak knives?" For some reason I see those commercials on TV, where the poor woman is trying to cut a tin can with her steak knife, and getting nowhere. Then the new steak knife from Japan comes along.

I can't take him seriously. Bears are not a cause for fear and alarm. Bears talk, and eat honey and picnic baskets. Winnie the Pooh, Smokey, Yogi – these are not scary pictures.

"Hey, there," I say. "What's your name?"

It yawns. The health bar is a gooey mess, lying on the ground. I peel away the shredded wrapper, and give the end of the health bar to the bear cub. It eats eagerly.

"Careful, Alan!" calls Victor.

– *His name is Carlo*, says Norbert.

"How do you know?"

– *I just do.*

"Well . . . hi, Carlo," I say. The bear licks its mouth and peers around the clearing.

"He's looking for his mother," says Victor anxiously.

"No, he isn't. He's looking for another health bar. Where is it, Carlo? Where's the bar? Can you find one? Come on, boy!"

The bear pads across the clearing and stops. I stop too. He moves forward, slowly, and scrabbles under a bush. I hold the bottom branch out of the way, and – there's a treasure trove. Two bars. I take them.

The bear looks up at me and whines. "Okay, Carlo," I say. "You found them." I open one bar and give half to the bear. He eats it in one gulp. I eat my half in one gulp too.

Victor rushes up. "Hey," he says. His mouth is open.

"Oh, okay, Victor," I say. I open the other bar and give him half. He eats it in one gulp. I eat the other half. Carlo whines. I give him the wrappers. He paws them.

"You got more than I did," says Victor.

The bear cub scratches himself, then sniffs the air.

"Come on, Carlo," I say. "Keep looking. Find a health bar for Victor."

He sets off through the forest, sniffing busily. Victor and I follow. A little procession through the northern woods. Three lost children.

We're moving downhill, through bare rock and scrub forest. Mostly we're in shade, but every now and then we come to an open area. Blue sky overhead. Through the trunks of the trees I can make out sunlight glinting on water. That's the direction we're headed.

Two health-bar-stops later, we come to a large clearing, and stop dead. In the middle of the clearing sits a trim and tidy log cabin. The door is shiny and red. The chimney is smoking cheerfully. The front step is swept clean. The window is polished. The window box underneath it is filled with flowers. The whole glade is sun-dappled and breezy. Behind the cabin is a lake. The water flashes silver through the trees.

"Where are we now?" cries Victor.

I know what he means. The picture is so perfect it seems fake. A scene from a fairy tale. I expect an elf or fawn to come trotting up and welcome me to the enchanted wood. But it's all real. I blink. The log cabin is still there.

Carlo is pawing at the red door. A little old lady opens it with a broom in her hand. "You again!" she shrieks. "Get away, now. Scat!" She brandishes the broom, and Carlo scampers off.

Then she notices us. "Bears are a nuisance around here," she says, frowning right at me. She's about my height, shorter than Victor. "So are campers." She closes the door.

"Wait!" We run forward. "Wait, please!" We pound on the door.

She takes a minute to open up. No broom in her hand now. She's holding a health bar. "What is it? Talk fast. I don't want to lose my light." She peels the yellow wrapper and takes a healthy bite.

9

Dwarves Who Didn't Make It

She's a colorful old lady. Not colorful like my uncle Emil, who likes to put on false vampire teeth and scare people. ("I vant to suck your blood, young man! *Mwah* ha-ha!" What an idiot.) This lady is literally colorful, like a rainbow. There are colorful stains on her face and wire-rimmed glasses. Paint, I guess. Flecks of color in her gray hair, which hangs in a braid beside her head. Smears on her hands and overalls. Drips on her boots. And what boots!

"So what do you want, boys?" she says.

Victor introduces us both. He's got good manners. I don't. I'm staring at her boots. The lady is small and delicate – kind of birdlike – but her boots are bigger than

Ronald McDonald's. No question, they were her foot-prints we were following.

"I'm Doris. Doris Appel," she says, and then pauses. I think we're supposed to recognize her name. We don't say anything.

"How'd you get here?" she asks. "Where's your boat?"

A natural question. Victor looks embarrassed. "We lost it."

"We were with my . . . with Christopher. A grown-up," I say. "We got lost on the portage. It wasn't our fault. We found some of those health bars."

"These bars!" She takes a bite of hers. "Good, aren't they? I found a pack of them while I was walking in the woods a while ago. I carried the pack home, and then real-ized there was a hole in the bottom. But I didn't see any grown-up."

"They were lying on the ground," I explain. "We fol-lowed them."

– *Like Hansel and Gretel. That's the story I meant. Not Davy and Goliath.*

"Quiet, Norbert."

– *Come on, Dingwall, the lady's got a broom – do I have to spell it out? You want us to wait in the gingerbread house?*

The old lady snorts. "You can't wait in my cottage. Visitors disturb my concentration."

"But you don't understand . . . ," Victor begins.

"It's not that I'm mean," she says. "Well, I am, but not usually like this. It's just that I'm in the middle of a

63

picture, and there's paints and turps everywhere. You boys can hang around out here until your friend comes. I'll even give you a snack. There's a few health bars left."

"But —" says Victor.

"No!" She holds up her hand.

Victor is flabbergasted. He's not used to grown-ups who won't listen to him. I am, but I don't know how to get through. I don't know how to talk to Doris Appel, whoever she is. Norbert clears his throat.

— *Oil paints, or acrylics?*

She frowns. "Oils, of course. I tried acrylics for a while, but I found that I just couldn't get the same —"

— *Depth*, suggests Norbert.

She's staring at me now. "Yes," she says. "Depth."

— *Oh, I agree entirely. Layering the colors over time gives a much more satisfying effect. Acrylics are too facile.*

She nods. "Facile is the exact word."

— *If I've said it once, I've said it a thousand times: acrylics are for ploshers. Nerissa has an acrylic in her whining room. She thinks it's a misterpiece, but I can't bear to look at it.*

I wonder what a misterpiece is. Does Norbert mean masterpiece? I hear a sound like distant bowling. Thunder?

Doris is smiling at me. "How do you know so much about painting?"

I don't know what to say. I shrug.

— *Well, I'm only a dabbler, you understand. Oils, and the occasional watercolor. But where I come from, painting is taken seriously. I'd really like to see your work.*

She looks pleased. Hesitates. Then throws up her hands. "Well, okay," she says. "I don't usually do this, but . . . you boys can come in. Be careful. Please be careful."

She holds open the door for us. She looks me up and down.

"You have two voices," she says. "Which is the real you?"

"Me," I say.

– No, me!

"Thank you, ma'am," says Victor, pushing past me. "Don't pay too much attention to Alan. He likes to make jokes."

She points across the room. "The pack with the health bars is over there under the big window," she says. It's our emergency pack all right.

"What's a whining room?" I say to Norbert.

Messy. Sticky. Smelly. They sound like some of the dwarves who didn't make it into the Snow White story. That's what the cottage is like inside. Bright enough, with a view of the lake, but the walls – the far wall in particular, on your left as you go in – are a mess of drips and smears. The floor is a minefield of gooey rags and ripped pictures and jars of paintbrushes. I can't imagine how she can find a place to put her size 37 feet. There's a sharp smell of smoke and turpentine. My eyes water. Pretty yucky.

The garden outside was a fairy tale – and I suppose this is too. Fairy tales have their yucky side. Imagine living in a shoe with an old lady who starved you and beat you.

A plain wooden table and chair are the only pieces of furniture in the room. There isn't even a bed. She sleeps in a sleeping bag on the floor.

– Great steaming mugs of cocoa! says Norbert. *What a wonderful picture!*

What's he see that I don't? I'm standing next to the far wall.

She's beside me, fiddling with something in her hands.

"Do you like it?" she says. "Do you really like it?"

– You've captured the subject perfectly. What apparency! What transilience! Mars, isn't it? Mars and Venus.

"Mars. Really? Why . . . I suppose it could be, Mars and Venus."

– And Saturn. And Pluto.

"Really?"

– And the Cocoa Jug. It's a real misterpiece!

She isn't paying attention. "I thought of calling it *Man and Woman.*"

– Why on Jupiter would you do that?

Victor's eating a health bar and staring out the window. There's a pair of high-powered binoculars on the table. He fiddles with them, puts them to his eyes.

"But you're right, Alan," says Doris thoughtfully. "Now that you mention it, I see that it could be Mars and Venus. You know, you're very mature for a youngster. I've never put a classical theme into my work before. The Arts Council will be impressed. They might even renew my grant."

I have no idea what she's talking about. I'm staring at the paint-spattered wall. Thousands and thousands of dabs of color. You know, I can see Norbert's point. All the little dots and streaks against a plain dark background. He's right. Forget the pictures; the wall *itself* looks like the night sky. Is that what he means about Mars and Venus? Maybe.

"What's that, Norbert?" I point at a big blob in the middle of the wall. "A comet?"

– *The Clam Nebula, of course. Nerissa looks for it every night.*

"What do you think of the frame, then?" Doris holds a picture in her hands. That's what she's been staring at all this time. The size of a small poster, and almost as brightly colored. "Should the frame be more ornate, if the painting has a classical title?" She holds it up. I notice what the picture is actually about. Oh, my gosh!

– *Hey, they've got no clothes on!* says Norbert.

I start to giggle. I can't help it. I'm pretty embarrassed. There's another picture on the far wall, and a bunch more stacked on the floor. I check them out.

Whew! Not a shirt or pair of pants in sight.

"What's wrong?" asks Doris. "I'd call it a perfectly natural expression of feeling."

– *I'd call it bathtime!*

I giggle some more.

She hangs the picture on a nail and stands back. There's her name at the bottom right. DORIS APPEL.

— *Now I can't see the Milky Way*, says Norbert.

"HEY!" Victor's on his feet, the binoculars at his eyes. "THERE'S MR. LEECH!"

I stop giggling. Naked people aren't funny anymore. I run over. "Where?"

My heart is beating. Well, I know it is, but what I mean is, I can feel it beating. Like a pile driver. I peer out excitedly.

The window looks out over the end of a lake. Most of the right-hand side of the window shows open water. Looking to the left, I can see where the water narrows and the land drops away. There's a small waterfall and the start of what looks like a river.

I don't see Christopher anywhere. Victor's got the binoculars pointed away from shore.

"Where?" I say. "Where's Christopher?"

"There!" He points into the middle of the lake.

"Huh?" I grab the binoculars from him, and focus them. Christopher's broad shoulders and thick head of hair jump into my view. He's in a canoe and paddling hard. But . . . but . . .

"But he's going away! He's going *away* from us!"

I'm really upset. All this time we were hungry and alone in the woods, I figured Christopher couldn't be too far away. The sight of him now . . . way out in the middle of the lake . . . getting farther and farther away. . . .

A grown-up leaving me is hard to take. Especially a grown-up *guy*. I know it doesn't make much sense, since I never liked Old Leech, but I can't help it. I feel like I've been kicked in the stomach. I keep staring at his broad stupid backside. I shout at him to come get us. I know he can't hear me, but I shout anyway.

"What's going on?" asks Doris. "What's wrong?"

"Our grown-up," I say. "Christopher. My . . . my mom's . . ." I can't say it.

"He's paddling away without us!" says Victor.

"Where'd he get the canoe?" I ask. "Did he steal it?"

"It's our canoe," says Victor. "I recognize it. He must have found it back in the swamp."

"But then he *knows* we're still here," I say. "That makes it worse!"

"He must be going to the summer camp for help," says the lady. "Oh, dear."

She explains about the camp. It's on the other side of the lake. "A long paddle," she says. "I go over myself, for groceries, every other week. I should have gone yesterday, in fact, because there's nothing to eat now except those health bars."

She starts rummaging around the room. I focus the binoculars over Christopher's head. I see buildings on the far shore of the lake.

"What'll he do at the camp?" I ask.

"He'll use their phone," she says. "There's a ranger station near Kawartha. They'll put out an alert."

Victor gulps, embarrassed at the thought of all that attention.

"They'll send helicopters and searchers after you."

69

Victor shakes his head.

"They'll phone your parents."

"My parents? My mom?" I can't tell how Victor feels about his parents finding out. His face is twisted up.

"They'll disrupt my routine," the lady says. "I have only another week up here, and then I have to go back to the city. I do not want my last days of peace ruined by noise and alarms and rude people asking questions. *Ahh!* There's my purse."

It's a big hairy sack, a cross between a pillowcase and a Pekinese dog. She reaches inside and finds a cell phone. Victor relaxes. I relax. A symbol of civilization, of normalcy. Everything will be fine now.

Or will it? She punches the number, waits. "Hello?" she says. "Hello? Hello?" She peers at the front of the phone. "Drat," she says. "Drat drat drat!"

"Low battery?" I say. I have a cell phone myself – a gift from my dad – and it's always running low.

She nods. Puts away the phone. Goes over to a hook on the wall and puts on a life jacket.

"What's going on?" I say.

She fastens the belt up, puts on a helmet, and turns around to face us. I try not to look at her boots.

"Because the stupid cell phone has run down," she explains, "I can't phone the camp to tell them about you. So I'll have to go over myself. Two hours hard paddling."

"Can we come too?" says Victor.

"It's a kayak," she says. "There's only room for one."

"Don't you have a motor boat?"

She shakes her head. "This is a protected lake. No power boats allowed."

"I still don't understand," I say. "Why not charge up your phone? That'll be easier than paddling across the lake."

"How, Alan?" She grabs a paddle from the floor. And drops it. It falls with a clatter. She swears, and bends down again. "I'm always doing that," she says.

It's not like a canoe paddle. It has two blades, one on each end. She grabs it in the middle, looking a bit – a very little bit – like the Death Maul character in the *Star Wars* movie. She smiles grimly at me. "How can I charge up my phone? There's no electricity in this place."

"What?" says Victor.

I look around. No outlets. No lightbulbs. There's a few of those oil lamps with wicks. You've seen them around – usually for decoration. Here they're for light.

"I don't see anything else to do," she says. "I'll paddle across the lake and send help back for you boys. You stay near here. If you're hungry, too bad. There are some blueberry bushes down by the rapids. Probably not too much fruit left, but you never know. Don't fall in – it's slippery."

"No, wait," I say. I stare at her. Doris Appel. A grown-up. A part of me – a little part of me – doesn't want to see her go. Don't leave! Don't leave me! "Bye," I say at length.

"Bring back some food," says Victor. He shakes out the emergency pack – two bars left.

"Hey, I get one!" I cry.

– *Thank you!* says Norbert.

"Yes, thank you!" says Victor.

71

Don't leave me, I plead silently.

She nods good-bye, closes the door behind her. A moment later we see her down by the water, climbing into her kayak. She wobbles, getting her feet in, and drops the paddle again. When she finally pushes off, she's surprisingly graceful. Her stroke is smooth and circular, propelling the boat quickly. The broad blades flash across the water like a dream of flying.

10

Girl in a Boat

"What's wrong? Why is she moving so slowly?" Victor and I are at the window. I've been staring at the same pointy boat shape for five minutes now, and it hasn't moved.

"What?" Victor has the binoculars. I repeat my question.

"Her? The kayak went behind the land there a while ago. I'm looking at a duck now."

I take the binoculars from him, and, with a little trouble, find what I was staring at. What I thought was our artist lady is really a sunken tree, with dead branches sticking out of the water. I've been urging it onward, wishing it all sorts of good luck, for the past five minutes.

I turn the glasses, trying to find Victor's duck.

"When do you think she'll get back?" he asks.

"Soon, I hope. I'm hungry."

"Me too."

I put down the glasses. We stare at each other.

— You know, that picture doesn't show the constellation of The Microphone very well. The Big Boot is good, but a bit too far below the East Star.

"Norbert, that isn't a picture at all," I tell him. "It's just drips on the wall."

— Oh, yeah? Look at the spur on the Little Boot. I'd like to see you do better!

"Alan, why do you talk about crazy stuff? The Microphone and Little Boot are not constellations."

I've given up trying to explain about Norbert. "Sorry," I say. "I can't help it."

Neither of us mentions the pictures of naked people. I think we're both embarrassed. All that naked flesh. Fronts and backs, tops and bottoms. It's safer to stare at the drips on the wall.

"How about going outside for some blueberries?" says Victor.

"Good idea."

We make sure to leave the door open. Don't want to be locked out if it starts to rain. And it looks as if it might. It's still sunny, but there's a huge thunderhead sailing towards us.

"She said the blueberry bushes were down the rapids," says Victor. "This way." He leads; I follow.

The cabin is built near a rocky point. On one side of the rocks is a pebble beach. The open lake laps gently at the shore. Actually, the wind is picking up and the water is lapping hard now. The artist lady launched her kayak from here. I peer into the distance, but of course I can't see her. There's another thunderhead sailing past. That makes three I can see. They're tall tall clouds, with flattened tops. I know they're the kind that bring storms, but they don't look dangerous. They float silent and serene, like balloons.

It occurs to me that I have no idea what blueberry bushes look like. The only blueberries I have ever seen were inside muffins. Somehow, I do not think I am going to find a dozen muffins growing wild.

The rapids start on the other side of the point. The lake narrows down, so that it looks like a river, and the land falls away. There's a bit of a waterfall, and some big rocks. The water moves fast. The rapids look scary to me – the water runs white, and the spray splashes high in the air. I pick up a twig and throw it in the water, watch it smash against a boulder and disappear into the spray.

"Hey, Alan. Come here!"

Victor is down the rapids, waving.

"What is it?"

"Blueberries!"

I hurry towards him.

They say there's nothing to beat the taste of fresh-picked fruit. Whoever *they* are. Well, they're wrong – at least about blueberries. I pick and pick and pick, and end up with a handful of dirty dark pills. They taste okay, but I'd rather have a muffin any day.

And it's hard work. The bushes are low to the ground, so the berries are tough to get at. This late in the year, there aren't that many. Victor and I clamber farther and farther downstream, leaning way out from the top of the bank. The water looks deep, and it's moving quickly. Boulders, eddies, lots of spray. A big piece of a tree floats past me, hits one of the boulders, flips over, and disappears underwater.

"Do you think we're in the right place?" I ask.

Victor points to some damp mud beside a nearby pine tree. There's a footprint the size of a tennis racket. Doris has been here.

When we hear the shouts, we both jump and stare upstream. Is it her?

No.

"What the . . . ," Victor says.

A silver bullet heads towards us. It's not really a bullet, of course – it's a canoe. With a single paddler, working like fury, aiming right for the heart of the rapids.

Not Doris. Not Christopher, either. The paddler is wearing a helmet, and a yellow life jacket.

The canoe is surrounded by foaming water. Looks like it's heading for the same rock the log hit earlier, but at the last minute the canoeist leans back hard on the paddle, and the boat shoots up away from the rock and across to the side of the river. Our side. I can see the paddler clearly. It's a girl, not much older than I am. The silver canoe is marked with a sign I've seen before – like an upside-down horseshoe. I can't remember what it means.

She sees us, gives a fierce grin. Her teeth are very white in her tanned face. She waves her paddle at us. "Wahoo!" she shrieks, skimming off down the rapids. I crane forward to follow her through the rising spray. She fends off one boulder with her paddle, and swings the canoe around behind another one, using it as a breakwater. She sits in still water a moment, then darts away, negotiating the rest of the rapids with ease and emerging from the splash and spray into a stretch of gentle current farther downstream. She turns in her seat to look back, waves her paddle one more time before another set of rapids carries her around the next bend. I stare after her. It's as if she is a mythical creature, a force of the wilderness, part girl, part canoe, as the centaurs were part human and part horse.

– *Ahem*, says Norbert.

"Wow," I say. "Isn't she something!"

"I'll say," says Victor.

– *Yeah, yeah*, says Norbert. *Girl in a boat. Big deal. Say, don't look now, but there's a fly in the cabin. A couple of flies, actually. Big ones.*

"Something in the cabin?" says Victor. "It couldn't be her, could it?"

– *It's flies, I tell you.*

Could Doris be back yet?

"Let's go," says Victor.

We scramble back the way we came. I almost fall in. "Careful!" says Victor. "You don't have a life jacket on."

As if that would save me from the rocks! I imagine myself bobbing downstream in perfect, supported comfort, safe except for a completely crushed skull.

The cabin is in view, and . . . can it be? "Look in the window!" I cry. "It's her!"

There's certainly someone there. I can see them moving around. "Hello!" I say. "Come on!"

We run right up to the fairy-tale red front door of the cabin. It's still open. I'm in the lead. I charge inside, and stop dead.

Victor stumbles in after me, bumping into me. "Hello!" he pants. "Thanks for . . ." His words crumble and blow away like ashes.

Two intruders. I recognize one of them.

"Carlo?" I whisper. My voice catches in my throat. Oh, yes, it's Carlo. He cocks his head and ambles towards me. He must have come to find more of the health bars. They *are* tasty.

I guess I'd be happy to see him if he were alone. But he's not. He's brought his mom with him. Her I can do without. She's busy ripping the emergency pack to shreds.

Next thing I know, Victor and I are running through the woods. "That was close, back there!" he gasps. "Good thing you remembered to close the door. You're so smart, Alan. Brave, too!"

"Aw, shucks," I say.

No, wait. I'm ahead of myself again.

11

She Belongs Here

Next thing I know I'm frozen in place. I can't move. I can't talk.

"This is not good," Victor says, in a throttled whisper. "It is not good at all." He sounds like the fish in *The Cat in the Hat*.

The big bear makes a deep snuffing grunt, and opens her mouth wide in a yawn. This is not a cute bear. She's not wearing a hat. She's not going to make jokes, or sing songs. Her eyes are crossed. One of her ears is hanging down in bloody strips. Her fur is dirty and matted.

Carlo keeps rubbing against me. His mother growls. Is she mad? I hope not. She's terrifying. Big as a small horse, and – I don't know how else to put it – *old*. Not old like your very first pair of shoes, or old like your granny, but old like the biggest tree in the park. I get the impression that she and her kind have been around this part of the world – the wild part: forest, swamp, and river – almost forever. That she belongs here, and the log cabin doesn't. Victor and I certainly don't.

"Don't run!" hisses Victor. "Whatever you do, don't run. Bears can run as fast as a racehorse."

I have a momentary image of bear racing, with the winner eating the jockey. I shiver. The big bear stares at her cub and then at me. Her head is on one side. Her mouth is open. Her teeth are as long as my fingers, and needle-sharp at the end.

I still can't move. That's what happens to me when I panic. I stay still.

"Don't make her mad. Don't get between the cub and the mother," whispers Victor. He's got lots of advice about what not to do. I can't even nod to say I understand. I feel like that prehistoric guy they found in the ice.

– *On Jupiter we call them flies.*

Oh, no. Quiet, Norbert, I think to myself. Just be quiet about bears and flies.

"What are you doing, Alan?" whispers Victor.

– *Because, of course, that's what we do when you run into them. Do you understand, Dingwall? Hey, Dingwall? Are you listening?*

Oh, dear. "Yes, I'm listening," I whisper. "You *fly* from them. The way you *bear* the flies. Yes, I get it."

"Shut up, Alan. Shut up and let's get out of here."

The mother bear peers in our direction. She's fifteen feet away. I can smell her. Not pretty, let me tell you. She begins to rub her back against the wall.

I can move now. Talking to Norbert broke the spell.

The bear comes down on all fours again. The cabin shakes. My heart is racing. I'm trembling, breathing quickly, ready to . . . I don't know what.

– *Run!!! Run! Run!!!*

That's it. Victor screams, and runs through the door. I turn tail and follow. The floor shakes. The bear is coming after us.

Next thing I know, we're running through the woods. Fast as we can. I hear crashing behind us. Bears? I hope not. I don't look. The river is on our right. The path is very uneven. I stumble, pick myself up, and keep running. My legs are wet from the river spray.

"That was close, back there!" gasps Victor. "Did you remember to close the door, Alan?"

"Um," I say.

"You're so . . ."

"Smart?" I offer. "Brave?"

He trips over a root, and grabs on to me. We teeter on the edge of the riverbank.

"So idiotic," he says.

We fall into the river together.

I was hot, and now I'm not. But I don't feel relieved. The water moves swiftly, carrying me along with it. I use my feet to push off one rock, only to bash into another one going backward. I bounce off awkwardly, so that I end up sliding downstream feetfirst. After I bump into three rocks in a row, I'm glad I'm going feetfirst. I'd hate to be fending them off with my head.

I spot Victor, slightly ahead of me. He's swimming easily, with slow steady strokes, letting the current take him downstream. He's okay. I'm okay. Our moms would think we were in danger, but we're way better off than we were just a few minutes ago.

Now I have time to feel relieved.

– *Whee!* cries Norbert. *This reminds me of rides on Jupiter. Only, of course, our water is a different color.*

Not my first dip today – I fell in, loading the canoe. Was it only this morning? I feel years older.

"Was that all your idea?" I ask Norbert. We slide down a tiny waterfall. Kind of fun. "Screaming like that to get us to run?"

– *Well . . .*

"Thanks. I think."

The dark green treetops make an interesting pattern against the blue sky. We slide by quicker than I could run. The water bends to the right, and widens out. We slow to a walking pace. I put my foot down, to try and stand up, but the current is still strong enough to knock me off my feet. I do a somersault, and end up with my feet out in front of me again. Just as well – a boulder looms. I fend it off.

The sun is shining directly on my face. It's been on my face a lot today. I wish I'd brought sunblock. And I'm not the only one.

– *Whew, I'm getting hot,* says Norbert. *Do you have air-conditioning?*

"I really don't know," I say. "Look around in there. Whatever you can find."

The water is really slowing down now. The trees on my right slide by in a relaxed, leisurely style. Lots of little eddies and ripples. The bank on my left is lower, and the ground is flatter. Fewer trees, more reeds.

The water is a different color. I'm sure it's the same water as before, but when it was splashing over rocks and boulders it looked clean and clear. Now it looks green and dirty.

Victor is staggering through the shallows, towards the left bank.

– *Careful,* calls Norbert. *I saw a shiver over there.*

Victor pauses. "A shiver?"

– *We call it a shiver on Jupiter. You know, one of those long thin things. Hisses at you. Alan fell asleep near one just a while ago.*

"A snake? You saw a snake on the bank over there?" He draws back.

– *Actually, it was in the water.*

Victor hurries out on the right bank. I catch up to him and start to clamber out.

"Careful," he says. "It's slippery."

83

"Yes, if I fell that would be horrible, wouldn't it? I might get . . . wet."

"Shut up." He almost smiles.

The land slopes upwards towards the pine woods. I don't want to climb the hill. My clothes hang wet and heavy on me. I'm hungry. "Now, what?" I say.

"I don't know. I wish Mr. Leech was here. Or the old lady. They could tell us which way to go."

"I thought you were a camper," I say. "Don't you know what to do on your own?"

"I've always had someone tell me what to do."

"Oh."

– *Go to the right*, says Norbert. *And do it now!*

The river bends that way. We won't be climbing. Sounds as good as anything else. Victor brightens. "Okay," he says, marching away.

"Do you have any idea where we're going, Norbert?" I ask in a whisper.

– *Shhh. Just keep going.*

Funny thing. I feel better too. I like having someone else do the directing.

"Careful here," Victor calls to me. "The ground is uneven. You might twist your ankle."

"Yes, Mom," I say. Just before he smiles, I catch a glimpse of longing on his face. He misses his mom.

"Look, up ahead!" Victor points. Something is glinting on the rocks.

"Is it a bird? A plane? Christopher?" Not, you understand, that I think he's Superman.

We run towards it. The glinting becomes clearer. It's a canoe.

Actually, it's half a canoe, scarred and dented. It sits on top of a stump, like an aluminum hood. Someone has nailed a sign to the stump: BEARCLAW RAPIDS it says. Underneath is the horseshoe symbol, like the one on the canoe-girl's boat.

Scary, to think of the water being that violent, that strong. I think how lucky we are to have come down the rapids uninjured.

"Is it – *hers?*" Victor clasps his hands together on the word. "Please let it not be . . . *hers!*" Great galloping gophers, the boy's in love.

– Oh, for heaven's sake, says Norbert.

It's sunny, but some gray clouds are moving in, like a gang of bullies trying to take over the sky. Sometime soon there's going to be one heck of a storm.

I feel an overwhelming sense of the size of the wilderness. I see hills and river and rock and mud; I see trees, and more trees, and more trees, rising all around me. Beyond them, the hills and sky. My footprints in the mud, like the broken canoe, are faint and fragile symbols of human intrusion. They are my link with my own kind. I begin to climb. Mud gives way to rock, and the footprints disappear.

"I'm really hungry," says Victor, limping after me. "And I have a blister. And it's getting later and later. We should make camp."

"What do you mean, 'make camp'?"

"Well, we should stop, and set up our tent and light our fire and cook dinner."

I stare at him. "Victor, we don't have any of those things."

Is that a rumble of thunder, off to the right? It's still sunny.

"No food," I say. "No tent. No fire. No dry clothes."

"I know." He sits down, and bows his head. At least he's not delusional. "I wish I was back home," he says.

"Me too, but that isn't going to help us now."

"Wish I hadn't come at all. It's . . . 5:30. Dinnertime. Mom'll be cooking pot roast, or something."

Yes, definitely thunder. "I wish I knew what to do now," I say.

"Me too." Victor starts to cry. His face puckers up, and his shoulders start to move.

Not good. Can it get worse? Yes, it can always get worse. But it doesn't – not this time. It gets better.

– *Look*, says Norbert.

"Where?"

– *Over there. I'm pointing.*

"Norbert, I can't see you. Where are you pointing?"

– *Over there. Come on, Dingwall. You can't miss it.*

Victor doesn't look. He probably thinks I've cracked up – talking to myself. I scan the horizon . . . and I see it. My heart jumps a beat. "That's smoke!" I shout.

A thin trickle, wafting above the trees. It's downstream from us, not very far away.

– *Yup.*

I can't tell you how it feels to realize that I'm not alone in the middle of the wilderness. Someone out there – someone nearby – can make fire. May not sound like much, making fire, but it's more than I can do right now. Fire is a powerful and positive achievement. I know – I *know* – that the person responsible for the fire is a good person.

"Come on, Victor – this way." I pull my friend to his feet, and drag him over mud and rocks, following the riverbed. The smoke is whitish in color – distinct against the dark bank of clouds.

The ground is very uneven. We have to jump over a deep cut made by – I don't know what. Groundwater, maybe.

I can see the campfire now. The flames are yellow and vibrant. We struggle closer, closer. Victor's blister makes him hobble. I help him along. He hangs on to my arm.

"Hello!" I call. "Hello!" No one responds. There doesn't seem to be anyone around the campfire.

"Help!" calls Victor. "We need –"

He trips, pitching forward and carrying me with him. We tumble together down a muddy gully. I end up on my back. A little stream runs down the gully, right underneath me. In fact, I am lying in the little streambed. It's very uncomfortable.

"You okay?" I ask Victor. He's beside me. I shake his arm. He groans.

"Yeah. Me too."

That's when I hear the laughter. Peal after peal, coming from above.

12

I Never Kid

The laugher stands straight and tall, silhouetted against the blue sky. A powerful hunter figure: muscles rippling, bow drawn, arrow pointing right at me. Scary and impressive at the same time. The figure looks like something out of mythology: Hercules, say. Or Thor.

Only she's a girl. "You are funny!" she says, lowering the bow. Her shoulder-length hair is a little darker than Thor's – about the color of light brown toast. Her eyes flash like gems. I don't know what kind of gems because I can't tell exactly what color her eyes are. I never understand how the people in books always know right away what color everyone's eyes are. I've known my mom all my life and all I can tell you about her eyes is that there are two of them and she puts glasses on them to read.

"I wondered what all the noise was. I came hurrying down. But you are only boys!"

This girl's eyes are bright. That much I can tell, even from down in my hole.

"Oh, hi!" I say. I recognize her. So does Victor. He's staring up at her in a trance. His mouth opens and shuts. His lips stick out. He looks like a fish, drowning in air.

"Remember us?" I say. "We were on the riverbank a while ago. You went past us in your canoe. You paddle really well."

She wears camper shorts and a T-shirt with the arms ripped off. She carries a knife as well as a quiver of arrows in her belt. Her arms and legs are tanned and muscular, and she has a rose tattooed on her calf. I can see it clearly, peeking above her work boot, because my head is just below the height of her work boot. I don't think Thor would have a rose tattoo. Hercules, maybe. You hear a lot of stories about those Ancient Greeks. . . .

"Did you see me run the rapids?" she says. "Wasn't it glorious? I've been trying all summer. There're only three of us at the camp who can do it. Me and two counselors. Trixie can't do it." Her face darkens on the name. "She broke her canoe in half."

She slips the bow over her shoulder, and bends down to offer us a hand each. Large hands, with thick strong fingers. Victor's hand trembles as he puts it in hers. She smiles fiercely and straightens up, pulling the two of us out of the gully as easily as I'd pull a couple of popsicles out of the freezer at the corner store back home.

She's older than I am, but not by too much. She's a head taller and a shoulder broader. The air around her is charged, as if there's electricity coming off her. When she breathes in, there doesn't seem to be enough air left for me.

"Thanks," I say. "My name is Alan. Alan Dingwall. This is my friend Victor."

He makes a sound like a dog throwing up.

"I am Zinta Zeeler!" she says. "My parents named me after the Zeletic goddess of death and destruction."

"Mine named me after my grandpa," I say.

I look around, expecting to find campers and counselors, or whoever it is she's camping with. I see the fire, and a small tent. I don't see any other people.

The wind is starting to pick up. I'm aware of my wet shirt sticking to me. "Could we . . . dry ourselves at your fire?" I ask. "And maybe get something to eat? You don't have any soup, or anything, do you?"

"Come," she says.

I nudge Victor. "Hey, loverboy!" I say.

He gazes over in her direction. "Doesn't she have beautiful eyes?"

"What color are they?"

"Why, they're . . ." He stops to think.

I tell you, the guys who write those books are just making it up.

The fire is roaring in the wind. I move close and hold out my hands to it. An elemental force. "Thanks," I say. "We really need your help here. You're from a camp, right?"

"Yes. I am staying at Camp Omega."

"Oh, that's great," I say. "We need to get to your camp right away."

"You can't," she says.

"You don't understand. We're hungry and tired. We've lost Christopher, my mom's . . ." I don't know if "friend" is the right word. "Our trip leader," I say. "With any luck, the rangers are looking for us. We've escaped from bears. You have no idea of our plight."

I don't know if "plight" is the right word, either, but I'll try it.

"No, *you* don't understand," she says. "Have you heard the thunder? Do you feel the wind? It would take me three hours hard paddle to get back to camp. Sunset in two hours. I will not risk traveling in the dark."

"Do you have a phone?"

"No."

"Oh. Well, who's with you now?"

"I am alone," she says. "I must spend the night away from the camp in order to complete my qualifications for the Master Tripper Award. Only two campers in the history of Camp Omega have been awarded the Master Tripper Scroll. I will be the third. And you boys will *not* stop me."

I take a breath. "Okay, let me see if I have it right. This Omega is a regular camp, right? Like in the Disney movies, with cabins and archery and a dining hall, right?"

She nods.

"And there are grown-ups too: nurses and counselors and camp directors?"

She nods.

"But because you're trying for this Girl Scout merit thing –"

"Master Tripper Scroll!" She makes it sound like the Victoria Cross.

"And because of this badge –"

"Scroll!"

"Whatever. Because you're in line for this award, you are here, alone, hours from camp. And no one is coming to get you until tomorrow."

She throws a log on the fire. It lands perfectly, and bursts into flame. "Yes," she says.

"Wow. Well, what do you say, Victor?"

He stares at me. I get a sense of the old Victor coming back. "I'm hungry," he says.

You can't fight your nature. Actually, I'm hungry too. I rub my hands together. I wonder how much food Zinta has. I could probably eat it all myself. Usually I'd feel bad about imposing on a stranger, but Zinta isn't the sort of person you have to feel bad about. She can look after herself.

"So, do you mind if we stay for dinner? We don't have anywhere else to go."

"Of course you will stay. You are not fit to look after yourselves, you boys."

Well, she doesn't have to put it like that. But I suppose she's right. "So, what did they give you for dinner?" I ask. "What's in the food pack?"

"Nothing," she says.

"What?" Victor's face darkens. The goddess girl has lost points. "You don't have anything in your food pack?"

"It is a survival exercise," she explains. "A true Master Tripper can live off the land. For my out-trip, I must find and cook my own food. The only things in my food pack are salt and pepper and a bit of flour. Good news, though. I have some gear in the canoe. Rod, reel, and a bucket of worms I dug up. You boys can come with me. This time of day, and with this wind, the fish should be rising nicely."

"You're kidding," I say.

She folds her arms. Her biceps bulge. "I *never* kid."

You know, she probably doesn't.

13

Following the Fin

The open lake is too windy to fish in, so we're in a narrow stretch below the rapids. It's still choppy. The canoe bounces up and down. The fishing rod in Victor's hand moves like a conductor's baton.

"Ready? Cast over towards the reeds!" calls Zinta. She's in the stern, paddling gently. Victor's in the bow. "Cast away!"

I have no idea what Zinta's talking about. I thought a castaway was someone stranded on a desert island. Victor flicks the rod back and forth, and lets fly. The line sails gently out. The boat rocks some more. The motion takes me back in time.

I remember the last time I held a rod in my hands, felt the living surge of the water beneath the boat, and smacked my lips over a fresh fish supper. I'm no fishing rookie. No, siree. I have, as they say, followed the fin. I have caught fish in my life.

Well, to be honest, I have caught one fish. I was small, and so was it. I figure it died of boredom on the end of my line. And if the day had lasted any longer, I'd have died of boredom in the boat. That was the last time I felt a rod in my hands – and also the first time. The fresh fish supper was at a restaurant, after none of us caught anything worth eating. The memories I am recapturing now are mostly hunger and seasickness, with a pinch of apprehension thrown in. There's no fish restaurant near Zinta's campsite.

I'm on the bottom of the boat, beside the worms. I'd feel sorry for myself, except that I figure the worms are even worse off than I am. At least I'm not being spitted on a hook by a laughing girl. Zinta seems actually to enjoy the . . . well, the brutal aspects of fishing. She keeps a club beside her, for bashing any fish we catch on the head.

Victor swallows nervously as he reels in. He doesn't want to look stupid in front of Zinta. And he doesn't want to make a mistake and miss catching a fish. If we don't catch anything, it's weed soup for dinner.

I'm not kidding. Weed soup. Zinta collected the weeds herself, from around the campsite. She told us the names of the weeds. The only one I remember is, "something like a nettle." Sounds yummy. There's a pot of this seething muck on the embers of the fire right now. She offered us a taste before setting out on our dinner-catching expedition. "Full of vitamins!" she declared. I said I'd wait.

Victor reels in slowly. And in. And in. And then the line stops.

"Snag," he says.

We drift quietly downstream. "Look!" I say. A big long-beaked long-necked bird stands on stick legs in the reedy shallows. It blends in well with the landscape. It belongs. Like the mother bear. It looks like it's been there since the river was made. As I watch, the bird bends down and grabs something with its beak.

"Wow! Did you see that?" I whisper.

"I can't get the hook out," says Victor. He wiggles the rod back and forth.

"Let me do it." Zinta stands up. The canoe wobbles slightly as she shifts her weight. The bucket of worms tips over. I reach out to grab them, and accidentally jostle the fishing rod.

"Watch it!" shouts Victor.

"Sorry," I say.

He reels in quickly now. The snag is gone. So is the hook.

"See what Alan did!" says Victor.

"No bother," she says, reaching into a pocket and pulling out a card with a bunch of hooks on it. "We'll put on another hook. Give me the rod."

The big bird takes off, ungainly, ponderous, its great wings beating. Something in its beak. I wonder what?

"You idiot, Alan. What did you knock against me for?"

"I said I'm sorry."

"Now Zinta thinks I'm a goop."

The big bird is right overhead now. Zinta is fiddling with her fishhooks. There's a flash of movement – something falling, a splash – and Zinta cries out, "Stupid bird!" She shakes her fist.

"What is it? What happened?"

She peers over the side. She's searching the water for something. Her eyes are . . . no, I still can't tell what color they are. They're angry, though. That, I can tell.

"Would you believe it?" she exclaims. "That big bird dropped a clamshell on me. Knocked all my fishhooks into the water. They sank."

"What'll we do now?" asks Victor.

She's frowning down at the fishing line. "If only we had something for the fish to catch themselves on," she says. "Something hook-shaped, and strong, and sharp."

Norbert clears his throat. I whisper to him to *shush*.

"Gee, I wonder," says Zinta.

Norbert clears his throat again. – *Grunewald's pocket*, he says.

"What?"

– *Come on, Dingwall, think. Grunewald's pocket. Something hook-shaped.*

What's he getting at? All Victor has in his pocket is a . . . Wait a minute.

"How about a safety pin?" I say.

"Shut up," he tells me. "Don't talk in that silly voice. And anyway, a safety pin is a stupid idea. . . . isn't it, Zinta?"

She shakes her head. "You know, it isn't stupid. Not at all. It's kind of smart. But where would we get a safety pin?"

We're drifting closer to the reeds. Zinta shoves us off. Victor digs into his pocket.

We all try our hands with the new hook. First Zinta, then Victor, then me. We catch exactly zero fish. I'm hungrier than ever. The rod in my hand is heavy. I cast towards the near shore. Zinta's line seems to float out forever, before sinking gently to the surface of the water. My line dribbles out about the length of my arm. "Sorry," I say. I reel in. I'm tired. While I'm yawning, I hear Norbert's voice.

– *Try the other side*, says Norbert.

"Huh?"

– *Cast over the other side of the boat.*

"But the fish are hiding on this side, in the reeds. That's where fish go."

– *Trust me. You'll do better.*

Victor frowns at me.

"Did you say something, Alan?" asks Zinta.

I shake my head, and cast on the other side of the boat. I do not do better. I let go of the line at the wrong time, and the hook goes straight up and straight down. The line is right under the boat now. "Sorry," I say again. "I –" And then I stop.

"I feel something tugging on the line," I say.

"There are some big fish around here," says Zinta. "Last year Trixie caught a record trout." Once again her face darkens. Trixie, whoever she is, is not a happy thought.

Zinta picks up her big club and taps it against her hand.

I pull again. And again. Nothing. "It seems to have stopped fighting back," I say.

"Probably another log," says Victor. I've already caught a couple.

I reel some more, and the line goes crazy. It shoots away from the boat, like a torpedo. I can't stop it. "What's going on?" I say. I stare stupidly at my departing line.

"It's a fish!" cries Zinta.

"It's dinner!" cries Victor.

"What do I do?" I cry.

"Hang on!" shrieks Victor. "Keep the end of the rod down."

"Don't pull too hard!" Zinta paddles furiously after the fish. "Don't break the line."

"Don't get tangled!"

I hang on grimly as the fish pulls away from the boat, and then across the front of the boat, and then away again. "He'll get tired," says Victor.

"Me too," I say.

The fish jumps out of the water. I can see the line leading into his mouth. I can't see Victor's safety pin.

"Wahoo!" cries Zinta. "Look at the size of it!"

I've never seen a fish like this. I almost drop the rod.

"Pull harder," says Victor.

"But not too hard," says Zinta.

– *Don't use too much water*, says Norbert.

What is he talking about?

– *When you're cooking the fish. And don't forget the salt.*

The fish jumps again. Not as high this time. It's getting tired. Zinta puts the club in her teeth, like a pirate. She paddles us over to the fish, which is thrashing around in the reedy shallows. I can't reel in anymore. I don't know what to do. The fish is on the surface. The water is all frothy. As we glide up to the fish, Zinta drops the paddle, snatches the club from between her teeth, leans over the side of the boat, and whacks the fish as hard as she can.

The boat wobbles. The fish is still struggling. Zinta whacks it again. And again. Her expression is triumphant. The Master Tripper look. She reaches down and grabs a flap of gill. Her arm muscles bulge when she lifts the fish from the water.

"Great job, Alan," she says. "You are a hero. We're going to have a grand supper!"

Victor sniffs. "It was my safety pin," he says.

14

Whup!

It's amazing how one little event can change everything. And I don't mean one little event like a teeny-weeny bubonic plague germ that happens to wipe out your town. I mean a little event like catching a fish. There I was in the boat, feeling pretty darn low – sorry for myself, and sorry that I was on this stupid camping expedition. Worried about Christopher and the old lady, and wondering what was going to happen to me. Would it rain tonight? Would we find Christopher tomorrow? Would we get home? Night was coming and we had no place to stay and nothing to eat.

There's the key. Nothing to eat. That's what changed, and it changed everything.

After something to eat – something in the shape of a huge bass, poached in not too much water for not very long, and served with salt and pepper and something called bannock, and horrible tea and all the second and third helpings you want, and no one worrying about table manners since there's only one fork between three of us – after all of that, I feel a million percent better. It helps that I am dryer than I have been in hours. It helps that I can stretch my legs. But it helps most that I am full.

"I love my independence," says Zinta. "This whole meal came from the land."

"Not the fish," I break in. "That came from the water."

Zinta frowns at me. I don't think she appreciates my sense of humor. Ah, well.

"Is there any more bannock?" asks Victor. Bannock is a kind of pretzel made with flour and water and salt. You loop a string of dough around a stick, and bake it in the fire. A charbroiled pancake.

"Sure, eat up," says Zinta. She's a good eater too. The muscles at the side of her jaw slide and bulge as she chews her fish. "Soup or tea, anybody?"

Victor declines politely. I shake my head vehemently. Nettle tea tastes like muddy socks, with a faint hint of gasoline.

After supper Zinta takes us up the hill near the campsite. A steep climb, me clinging on to pine trees, which are themselves clinging to the bare rock, with their roots outspread like fingers. From the top of the hill we can see a long way – north, I think. The thunderheads are piling up there. The setting sun is hidden behind clouds shaped like scoops.

"Oh!" Victor nods in comprehension. "So we're on an island!"

I can't see all the way around, but there's the open lake in front of us, and what looks like a bay to the right. That'll be the narrows, where the cabin is. I can't see the cabin. The rapids we bumped and tumbled down are behind us. I guess we are on an island, at that.

Victor is pointing down the lake. "And those lights at the far end are –"

"That's my camp. Camp Omega."

It does seem like a long paddle away. Too bad we can't get there tonight. I think about my phone conversation. *Hi, Mom! How are you? I'm fine. By the way, Christopher deserted us and we were nearly killed by rattlesnakes and bears.*

Zinta is frowning up at the sky. "It will be a dirty night. Look at those clouds." She clears her throat and gives a recitation:

> 'Mare's tails and mackerel scales
> Make tall ships carry small sails.'

"What?" I say.

"Haven't you heard that rhyme before, Alan?" says Victor. "It's famous. Like, 'Red sky at night, sailors' delight.'"

Zinta joins him for the tag line: "'Red sky at morning, sailors take warning.'"

"Oh, yeah," I say. "Now that you mention it, I think I heard that one on MTV. A rapper in a black leather sailor suit – what's his name? A.B. Sea? Ice Berg? Something like that."

A.B. Sea. You know, that's not a bad joke. Zinta isn't laughing.

"And how can it be a red sky at night?" I ask. "Sky's black at night, isn't it? The guys who make up these rhymes must never go outside."

Zinta ignores me. "It was a red sky this morning," she says. "My counselor was worried. Her barometer was falling too."

– *She should pick it up,* says Norbert. *Before it breaks.*

Now, this joke they get. I don't understand, because it isn't that great a joke, but they both start to laugh. "You are a funny one, Alan," says Zinta. Victor pats me on the back. I shrug my shoulders. Victor pats Zinta on the back. She turns in a heartbeat, grabs his wrist, and flips him head over heels in the air, so that he lands hard on his back. There's a *whup!* noise as the air goes out of him.

Wow. Not funny.

She stares down at him. "Don't *ever* touch me without asking."

Victor's mouth is wide-open, but he doesn't reply. He's trying to breathe. No point in helping him to his feet. I've had the wind knocked out of me before. Better to let him lie there and get his breath back slowly. I wonder how he feels about Zinta now?

She heads back down the hill at a run. We follow more slowly.

Time to move the canoe for the night. I go down to the water with Zinta. "Can I help?" I ask.

"How?"

"I could take one end," I begin, but she laughs and picks it up from the middle, all by herself. She balances it across her knee, with her hands on the thwart. The tendons in her forearms stretch against her skin.

I shrug. "Or I could sing a song," I say. "Yo ho, heave-ho, maybe?"

No reaction. She flips the canoe up and over onto her shoulders faster than I can flip a quarter. She trots up the hill to the campsite, canoe bouncing up and down. I run after her.

Victor pulls me aside. "Leave her alone," he whispers. "She's a monster."

I may be premature, but it seems to me that love has died. When you can call a girl a monster, you are no longer under the spell.

She puts down the canoe near the fire. "You two will sleep under there," she says.

"I hope you'll be comfortable in your warm dry tent," I say. I'm being sort of sarcastic, but she doesn't get it.

"Thank you. I shall be quite comfortable. The tent is lightweight and waterproof."

"And now?" I say. "Not that I think you're bossy or anything, but I just wondered if there was anything I should be doing at this moment?"

Does she know I'm teasing? Her face is as expressive as an orange. "Now, I will deal myself a few hands of cards, and you will clean up the dishes," she says.

"You play cards?" I say. "Can I play too?"

"After you do the dishes."

There are not a lot of dishes. One fork, two cups, one frying pan. We wash them in the river. Victor shows me how to use sand and mud for soap. This technique gets off the food, but the frying pan is black when we start, and still black when we get back to the campsite.

Zinta is sitting beside a flat rock with a deck of cards. She deals five cards, discards one card, and draws another. She's playing poker. She frowns at her new hand.

"What's wrong?" I ask.

"I was hoping to pick up a card that would finish the straight." She fans out her hand. "A straight is five cards in a row, like 7, 8, 9, 10, jack. A good hand."

"Yes, I know."

"I was dealt 7, 8, 9, jack, king. I threw away the king, hoping to pick up a 10 so I would have a straight."

"And you didn't draw the 10," I say.

"No. So now the hand is useless."

"Too bad. Could I make a suggestion?"

"I'm never going to beat Trixie," she says.

That name again. "Who's Trixie?" I ask.

Zinta shuffles the cards and deals again. You can tell by the way she shuffles that she does not have a lot of practice.

"Who," I ask again, "is Trixie?"

"It's bedtime," she says.

"About drawing to an inside straight," I begin. "You –"

"Shut up!"

I shut up.

15

The Bladder Rules

It is not wonderful under the canoe. With Zinta's waterproof groundsheet and spare blanket, we're not actually cold, but that's about all you can say for comfort. The groundsheet is ten feet long – just long enough for Victor and me to lie down end to end. I'm itchy and cramped, and there's a knobby root digging into my . . . well, my extreme lower back. Very uncomfortable, let me tell you.

The fire is down to embers. Zinta is rinsing and spitting somewhere nearby. The sky is dark. The thunder is grumbling, more insistently than it was earlier. "I thought it would be different," I whisper to Victor.

He's slapping halfheartedly at bugs and grumbling to himself. "What would be different?" he asks.

"The whole camping thing. I thought we'd stay up late, and sing songs under the stars, and tell ghost stories, and stuff like that."

"I'm too tired," he says.

"I thought at least we'd have hot chocolate," I say. I can feel the nettle tea in the pit of my stomach. I only had a few sips, but I suspect I'll remember them later. "Night, Victor," I whisper.

No reply.

"Hey, Zinta, want to hear a ghost story?"

No reply.

The water down below us is much noisier at night than it was during the day. I yawn, and swallow a flying thing. I turn over, trying to get comfortable. Victor is hugging the blanket tightly. The tree root is sticking into my left kidney. *Ouch.*

Zinta has a flashlight on in the tent. After a while it goes out. The campsite is quiet, except for that darn water and the bugs. And . . . something tromping around nearby. Something wearing army boots, it sounds like. I peer out from under the canoe. There's the something again, by the fire pit. It's a mouse. No, smaller than a mouse, a shrew. Honestly, the size of my baby finger. How can it make all the noise? "*Shhh,*" I whisper, and crawl back under the canoe. Now the tree root is under my right kidney.

I can't remember how I fall asleep, but I awake slowly and painfully, climbing up the ladder of consciousness one rung at a time. I do not want to be awake. I do not want to move. I want to climb back down into sleep, only – a big only – I have to go to the bathroom.

Can I wait? Sure I can. Can't I?

I scrunch myself into a ball, with my knees close to my chin. The feeling eases. I scrunch even tighter. I'm so tired. If I could just drift off to sleep, it'd be morning when I wake up. I feel sleep washing over me like a warm wave, carrying me away, but – a big but – I still have to go to the bathroom. Drat that nettle tea.

There is no bathroom, of course. I don't want to roll out from under the canoe, and shiver my way into the woods. I want to stay still. I want to stay warm. Mostly, I want to sleep. Every single part of my body is crying for sleep, except my bladder.

The bladder rules. I roll out from under the canoe.

Lightning flashes in the distance. Thunder rumbles. The wind *whooshes* through the pine trees. I creep away from the campsite, looking left and right, trying to find some privacy.

I'm self-conscious. I'm not used to going to the bathroom in the open. I know it sounds stupid, but I can't help feeling . . . exposed.

I find a bush. Check over my shoulder that no one is watching. The coast seems clear.

Okay. Unzip. Relax, relax, relax. And . . .

A lightning flash makes me jump. It lights up the campsite, and my bush. And me. I feel more exposed than ever. I want to be finished out here, but I can't even start.

I'm too nervous. Too close to camp. I zip up, and move farther away.

– *What's going on?* asks Norbert.

I jump again. "Geez, don't do that. You scared me."

– *What are you doing here?*

"What do you think?"

– *I don't . . . oh. Okay.*

I'm behind a tree trunk now. Thunder's louder than before. Storm's getting closer. Okay, now's a good time. I've got a little while before the next lightning strike. Now I can do it. Unzip again. Relax, relax. Ready, set, and . . .

A rustling noise from right overhead. I freeze, and run through a list of ugly possibilities. Bats, snakes, wildcats. There's the noise again. It's tree branches knocking against each other. *Whew!* Okay, I'm ready to try once more. Relax, relax. And . . .

– *Are you done?*

"No. Shut up."

– *Talk about your big production numbers.*

"Shut up. Just shut up!"

Deep breath. Concentrate. Relax. And . . .

"Who's that? Who's out there?" Zinta's voice, raised in a bellow.

I zip up in a hurry.

"I can hear you!" Zinta is shining her flashlight around the campsite.

I peer around my tree. "Hello," I say.

Flashlight shining right at me, blinding me. I put up my hand to shade my eyes.

She stands by the fire pit, knife in hand. When she recognizes me, she lowers the weapon.

"WHAT'S GOING ON?" she shouts.

"I was just trying to –"

"WHAT? WHAT WAS THAT?" She can't hear me. The wind in the pines is louder. "WHAT DID YOU SAY?"

Oh, for pity's sake.

I'm not going to be able to go to the bathroom now. I make my way back to the campsite. The wind almost knocks me off my feet. The trees are bending like hula dancers. Near the fire pit I stub my bare toe on the frying pan, and cry out in pain.

"Did you see something?" cries Zinta. "A bear? One of my counselors saw a bear on our way here. . . ."

And then, with me hopping on one foot, and the wind howling through the trees, and Zinta talking, I suppose, about Carlo or his mom, the storm breaks.

My bedroom at home looks out on Lake Ontario. When the wind is right, you can watch a thunderstorm like a TV show. Lightning shimmers and snakes down, thunder growls, rain marches across the lake, flattening the white-caps, before hitting our house.

I've seen lots of storms, but never one like this. Lightning flashes all around me faster than I can take it in: four or five strokes at once. I feel like I'm inside a microwave oven. Thunder hits right on top of the lightning, like the *crack* of a whip. Only this is more like four or five cracks at once: *SNAP-CRACK-HISS-CRACK!* Something hits my head. I stagger backwards. Water stings my neck and shoulders. I'm soaked before I even realize it's raining. I fall to the ground.

More lightning flashes. Zinta runs over. "Are you okay?" she asks. I cannot hear her, but I can read her lips. "Did the lightning hit you? It came right down."

We stare at the frying pan. Its handle droops now, as if it was . . . melted. The pan hisses when the rain hits it, steam rising.

My head hurts. "What's going on?" I ask. My voice sounds strange.

– *Great,* says Norbert. *Just great. Now the power is off in here, and I can't find the fuse box.*

"What were you doing?" Zinta demands.

We're in her tent, drying off with her damp towel. Just the two of us. Victor didn't want to leave the canoe. I don't know if he's scared of Zinta, or just tired.

"Why were you up in the middle of the night?"

"I had to go to the bathroom," I say.

"Oh. I wondered." She looks down, and I almost die. My checked shirttail is sticking out of my fly. I must have got it stuck there while I was zipping up in a hurry.

The tent is longer than it is high. No standing. I can sit cross-legged, and so can she. The flashlight hangs between us on a hook on the tent pole. It's dryer inside the tent than under the canoe, but not much. There's a good-sized puddle of water in the lower corner. In the light of the flashlight, I can see bugs flying around and landing on the ceiling and walls of the tent.

"You're a lucky guy, Alan. You could have died when the lightning struck."

"Yeah." I still feel weird. Like I'm someone else, as well as myself. The tips of my fingers and toes are numb.

Zinta's sleeping bag is open. Playing cards are strewn across the top. I finish with the towel, and hand it back.

"Want to play poker?" I say.

"Oh." She frowns. "Aren't you tired?"

There's a bug in my ear. I swat at it. "Right now I feel like I'll never sleep again."

She picks up the cards and shuffles them awkwardly. "Okay," she says. "I need the practice."

She deals five cards to each of us. I take a quick look at my hand. "Well, well," I say.

She frowns down at her own cards. "Would you like to draw any more cards?" she asks.

I shake my head. "I think this is pretty good," I say. "I've got all spades."

"Don't *tell* me," she frowns. "Don't you know any better? You're supposed to keep your hand a secret." She draws two cards, and sighs. "Well, I'd better fold," she says. "A flush – all one suit – is a good hand. I can't beat it."

"So I win?"

"Yes." She throws down her cards. The rain drums on the roof of the tent.

"I'll never beat Trixie," she says.

"Who's Trixie?"

She doesn't answer.

I reach for the spilled cards. Zinta starts to cry.

16

Between a Munchkin and a Mosquito

I'm flabbergasted – not a word I use much, but it fits here. Zinta is so very tough, so competent, so strong and in charge, that it's strange and, in a way, wrong to see her crying. Like watching your coach cry, or a librarian. You're used to them telling you what to do. "Pass the ball! Do ten layup drills! *Shhh!* Don't talk." Or a dental hygienist – they're tough, all right. "Rinse and spit!" they tell me, and I do. "Now hold still. This is going to hurt." And I do what they say, even though I don't want to get hurt.

I have *no* idea what to do now. In movies, when the girl breaks down, the guy always says, "There, there," and pats her on the cheek. I really don't want to do that to Zinta.

I'm afraid she'll revert into an action hero, and flip me onto my back. I don't say anything.

– *There, there*, says Norbert.

"*Shhh*," I whisper.

– *Good news, Dingwall. The power is back on. You must be feeling normal.*

Zinta chokes.

– *Tell us about Trixie*, says Norbert.

His voice sounds so whiny, so high and thin. A cross between a munchkin and a mosquito. I can't help wondering what Norbert looks like.

– *I'm sure she's a real stinker*, he says.

"Oh, she is, she is!" Zinta looks over at me. Her eyes are running with tears, and – I still can't tell what color they are because it's too dark. They're shining eyes. That much I can tell. Wet and shining and big. "She's so mean. Do you know what's going to happen if her stupid Trailblazers beat my Lumberjacks in the casino night games? Do you know? I was so stupid! I never should have dared her the way I did. *Ooh!* I couldn't bear to lose my Master Tripper Scroll. That little . . ." Zinta knots her fist and holds it up. Her knuckles are large and bony. I'm really glad I didn't pat her cheek.

– *Why don't we sit back and relax, and you can tell us all about it over a nice soothing cup of cocoa. Now that the power is back on, I can heat up my kettle. If only Dingwall had some air-conditioning.*

"Cocoa?" Zinta sniffs. "You mean nettle tea."

– *Heu heu heu!* Norbert laughs. *You and Dingwall can drink the tea if you want. I'll have cocoa.*

And Zinta's story comes out.

"It all began last year at camp," she says. Trixie – that's Trixie Mintworthy, from Rosedale, a ritzy part of Toronto – was in the Fox cabin and Zinta was in the Dove cabin next door, and the girls hated each other from the first. Trixie is rich and snooty, and Zinta is not. She calls Zinta "that yahoo" and "Tarzana of the forest." Actually, I think Tarzana suits Zinta pretty well, but she doesn't like the name. She calls Trixie "Little Miss Dainty."

There's a big games day at the camp. The whole place is divided into two teams: the Trailblazers and the Lumberjacks. Last year Zinta and the Lumberjacks won all the canoeing and archery, and Trixie and the Trailblazers won the swimming and tug-of-war and Red Rover. Then came casino night, and Trixie's team cleaned up. And the games day prize went to them.

"I said we'd get even next year," says Zinta. "I said we'd beat her in poker. And Trixie laughed, and pushed me. I hate people touching me. I always have. I punched her. It felt wonderful, smashing that pretty little upturned nose all over her face, but I got in trouble. And I had to apologize – that was the worst part. Trixie said she forgave me, and hugged me, and, when her face was near my ear, whispered that she was going to make my life miserable this year."

"And has she?"

"Oh, yes. Every time I go near anyone it's, 'Be careful, now!' or 'You have to watch out for Zinta. She can't control herself.' Makes me want to kill her. And on top of that. . . ." She stops. I don't pat her cheek. "On top of that, I was stupid. We're both trying for the Master Tripper Award this year. She said that if she lost the games, she'd give me her Master Tripper Scroll. I wasn't going to let her make a more generous gesture than me. I told her that if *we* lost the games, she could have *my* Master Tripper Scroll. Oh, I wish I hadn't!"

She clenches her fist. I slide away from her.

"The games begin the day after tomorrow, when I'm back. I should be pleased about winning the award. But now all I can think about is having to give it to Trixie."

There's a small silence when she's finished. I slap at a mosquito. She slaps at a mosquito. I'm getting an idea. "You know," I say, "without your help, Victor and I would probably be scared and starving in the wilderness right now."

She sniffs.

"I wonder if you'd let me help you, in return," I say.

"How?"

"I'm trying to figure it out." I yawn. "Maybe I am a bit tired after all. I think I'll be getting back to my canoe."

She opens her mouth, then closes it without saying anything.

"Oh, by the way," I fan out my poker hand, "I was lying. I didn't really have a flush."

She stares at my four spades and one club. "But, you said you did. You said you had all spades."

I smile at her. I don't say anything.

"And you didn't draw any cards."

I keep smiling.

"This is a bad hand," she says. "You shouldn't have won."

"But I did win. You folded your hand."

"If I'd known . . ."

"Yes," I say. "That's the whole point, Zinta. Night, now."

She's puzzled, and at a loss. I almost feel I can chuck her under the chin. Needless to say, I don't do it.

I go back to the canoe. Everything is soaked. Victor has all the blanket and most of the groundsheet. I grab my half back from him. He wakes up long enough to ask if the storm is over, then turns over and starts to breathe deeply.

I can't sleep. I feel tingly all over. I'm thinking about . . . lots of things.

– *You like her*, says Norbert.

"Who?"

– *You know who.*

Maybe that's what I'm thinking about.

– *Dingwall likes Zinta. Dingwall likes Zinta.*

"Oh, shut up."

– *What about Miranda? And Frieda?*

I don't know what he's talking about. Miranda is a friend from back home in Cobourg. Sure I like her, but she's just a friend. We might go bowling, or to the movies. That's all. Frieda is a girl I met this summer in New York

City. Another friend. I've never had a real girlfriend, and somehow I don't see Zinta as a good choice. Like going for a walk with a tigress.

Norbert knows about Frieda because he was there too. Which reminds me.

"There's something I meant to ask you before," I say. "How'd you get here?"

– *Everyone has to be someplace.*

"Yes, but I thought you were living on 84th Street in Manhattan. How did you get here?"

Victor kicks me in his sleep. I kick him back, and grab some of the blanket. It's chilly, and a wet blanket is warmer than no blanket at all.

– *Didn't you ask for help?*

"Did I?" I throw my mind back. Victor and me with the canoe on our backs, running, screaming. . . . "I guess so," I say.

– *I've told you before. You're never alone. You're never far from help.*

I smile into the dark. I can't help it. "Well, thanks, Norbert. I guess you're kind of a guardian angel, aren't you?"

– *One of these days, I may ask you for help*, says Norbert.

"Huh?"

– *It may be a little thing. I may ask you to wear more sunblock, for instance. It's really hot in here. Or it could be something bigger.*

"But . . . how could I help you? You live on Jupiter – millions of miles away."

– *I've helped you. Maybe you can help me.*
Not a guardian angel, after all. More of a godfather.

I lie awake in the dark, tossing around questions like a juggler tossing plates. Did I really get struck by lightning? Will the bears come back? Will we find Christopher? What happened to the painter lady? How will we get home? Why does Zinta draw to an inside straight? How does Victor sleep so soundly?

I can't answer any of my questions. The plates drop.

I feel strange – distant from myself, somehow. As if I'm on the outside of this whole adventure, drifting around, looking down at myself. Weird.

How close did that lightning come? I didn't feel it hit. I hold my hand close to my face in the darkness. Is it glowing? No. How many fingers am I holding up? Can't see.

Rain beating on the roof of the house or car can sound kind of soothing. Rain beating on a canoe, inches – no, millimeters – from your face, isn't soothing at all. For one thing, it's too loud. On the plus side, I can't hear any bugs, and I can't feel the tree root anymore.

The rain lightens up. From pounding, it turns into a gentle drumming, and then disappears altogether. Still tingling, I drift between sleep and waking, this world and some other one.

I'm at a space shuttle launch. For some reason the launch is taking place inside a garage. Two astronauts come out of a tunnel. No one else is around except me. One of the astronauts hops past me, but the other one stops. I move closer, to see the second astronaut's face. The helmet is mirrored. I can only see my own face, peering in at the astronaut. I lift one of my eyebrows. My left one. It's the only eyebrow I can lift. My reflection lifts his left eyebrow too.

Something wrong about that, but I can't figure out what. It all has to do with the second astronaut. Who is –

I wake up all at once, like falling into cold water. I never did go to the bathroom. If I don't go in ten seconds, I'm going to explode.

I just make it.

17

Mr. Rudipimpig

That's a relief. I squint at my watch. 6:57. I'm tired. My mind feels squishy. My skin hurts. My fingers are still numb. Victor and Zinta are already up. I can hear them. Victor is complaining about being tired. He should talk! He slept all night.

A bright windless morning. Not a cloud in the sky. I yawn, and scratch a bit, and wander back to the campsite. I wish I was cleaner. I wish I was sleeping. I wish I was home, come to that. Maybe with a big bowl of cereal and the comics. That Dilbert is a funny guy. If I were home right now, I'd have nothing to do all day except play and think about starting school soon. And avoid Christopher.

Do I wish Christopher was home with me? I do not.

Zinta has the tent down and rolled into a bag. She's checking around the campsite, throwing things into her pack. I spread the groundsheet out and roll it up into a tight ball. Well, a fairly tight ball. It's smaller than a car.

I hand the rolled-up groundsheet to Zinta. Without a word she spreads it out again, and rerolls it into a long thin tube shape. Her hands move precisely, like clockwork. When she's done, the bundle fits easily into her knapsack.

"Do you want me to start a fire?" Victor asks.

"Sure," says Zinta. "We'll have tea and get on our way."

She flips the canoe onto her back and carries it to the edge of the river. Victor bustles about, collecting armfuls of twigs and sticks. Then he gets down onto his hands and knees, and begins building a little tent of kindling.

I don't have anything to do. I close my eyes and listen to the sounds of nature. There's water, and birds, and bugs, and . . . something else. "Is that a helicopter?" I open my eyes, and peer around, but I can't see it.

"Probably from the ranger station," says Zinta, climbing back up towards me. She's wearing the same shorts as yesterday, with a different top. The front of her thighs divide into two groups of muscles when she strides. I never noticed yesterday. My thighs don't do that.

Victor is breathing hard. "I can't start the fire. The wood's too wet. Do you want to try, Alan?"

"Geez, Vic, I can't even get the gas barbecue to start at home."

Zinta laughs. I'm glad I can amuse her. She kneels beside the fire pit and twiddles with the sticks for a moment. Then she straightens up and tosses her hair out of her eyes.

"How did you do that?" Victor stares at the tongues of flame eating at the twigs.

"It's a knack," she says.

Victor feeds the fire the way a mother bird feeds her chicks – one stick at a time into its open red mouth. The fire is growing. A dense cloud of whitish smoke drifts straight up. The wet wood hisses and spits. I hold out my hands to the fire. If I were at home with Dilbert and a bowl of cereal, I wouldn't want a fire, but it works out here.

Voices carry well, over the water. There's a canoe coming downstream towards us. I hear a name echoing: *Zinta*. The people in the boat must be from the camp. There are two of them – older than we are. Counselors, I guess. They see her now. They call out excitedly. She waves and runs down to the water. I hear congratulations and cheers from the boat.

"Hey, Victor!" I say. "Forget the fire. Company's here!"

We clamber down, looking shamefaced and grateful. The two counselors are patting Zinta on the back. "We came early because we were worried," they say. "That storm last night was really something. You must have got soaked. Were you scared?"

Zinta laughs.

The counselors notice us. "Who are they?" asks the girl with dark bangs flapping under her helmet, and a sharp chin poking out.

Zinta explains. The counselors stare. "But . . . there are two missing boys. A man arrived at the camp yesterday. Zinta, is it them?" They turn to us. "Are you them?"

Them? Who?

"What are your names?" asks the other counselor. His helmet is dented. "The guy from the ranger station said . . ."

And then, from out of the eastern sky, invisible against the sun until the last minute, a helicopter appears. It drops towards us and stops, hovering directly over our heads. A bullhorn screams over the noise of the rotors.

"HAVE YOU SEEN TWO KIDS?"

Why should I think he's talking about us? But, somehow, I do think so.

"VICTOR AND ALAN! HAVE YOU SEEN TWO STUPID KIDS NAMED VICTOR AND ALAN?"

"Those are the names," says the counselor with the bangs. "The ranger was talking about them back at camp. Victor and Alan."

"Have you seen them?" asks the counselor with the dented helmet.

"We are them," I say.

The water is below us. The land too. Zinta and the counselors wave up at us from the campsite. The world spins away from me and back again, like some kind of private yo-yo. If there is a noisier, bumpier, more exciting, noisier, scarier, noisier form of travel than the helicopter, I don't want to know about it. And it's noisy too. I feel as if a thrash metal band is playing inside my eardrums. Takes my mind off my nausea, at least. I hardly feel sick at all.

Victor and I wear headsets like the pilot – earphones with microphones, so we can talk over the noise of the helicopter. Pretty cool. I feel like the teenagers who work at the donut drive-thru. Even with the headset, it's still noisy.

"We thought you were dead," grumbles the pilot. "With the storm last night and all. Best time to search for someone is right after they've been lost, and we couldn't search for you on account of the wind being too strong." His words echo in my headset.

We fly over the bottom end of the island, where it links back up with the lake. There's a beach, with lots of stuff washed up on it. I grab Victor's arm and point down. "Bears!" I say. A cub and a grown-up. Is it Carlo and his mom? They're wrestling with something that looks familiar. A pack. I can't be sure, but it might be ours. The cub has a bright red packet in his mouth.

"Scavengers!" says the pilot. "Wonder what kind of garbage they've found?"

I look at Victor. "Do you think it's our stuff?"

He nods. "Freeze-dried pork chops."

The helicopter spins sideways and heads across the lake. I try not to think about food.

"You stupid kids caused a lot of trouble," says the pilot. "You want to know how many choppers are out? Three. You want to know how much sleep I got last night? None. You idiots should know better than to wander off."

"We didn't . . . ," I begin, but the pilot interrupts.

"Right now I'm taking you to a summer camp across the lake," he says. "They've got medical staff and a heliport. Maybe next time you'll think twice before dashing away on your own! Now, what do you have to say to that?"

I don't know what to tell him.

– *You're a rude man*, says Norbert. Somehow the words get picked up by the microphone near my mouth, and transferred to the pilot's headset.

"Huh?"

– *Rude. And that's not all. You're dirty. And you have a big pimple on your forehead. It looks like it's going to explode.*

"Norbert, quiet."

The pilot seems to have something stuck in his throat. He chokes and swallows. I can't see all of his face, but what I can see is not happy. Oh, dear.

– *Yes, you are rude and dirty and pimply. And ignorant. I shall call you Ru-di-pimp-ig!*

"Why, you little –"

– *Sure, make fun of my size. That's easy. All I can say is, my airship travels a lot faster than yours, Mr. Rudipimpig. And I don't overshoot my landing.*

"What –" The pilot checks what he is about to say, and pulls back hard on a stick in front of him. The helicopter slows, turns around, and begins to descend towards a collection of wooden cabins and docks spread out along the far shore of the lake, and a swimming area marked with pretty blue and white buoys. Camp Omega, I presume.

18

Supermodel

"I'm fine, Ma. Fine. I really am. A bit tired is all. We were picked up by the rangers in a helicopter. What? I said a helicopter. No, not a doctor, a helicopter. Yes, there's a doctor here, and a nurse. I'm fine. I really am. I'm not hurt. I'm not hungry – well, maybe a bit."

Victor is talking on the phone in the infirmary. That's a new word for me – it means the camp hospital. It's a cabin with a couple of beds and a desk. And a phone. The infirmary is not a big place. With Victor and me and the doctor and camp director and the guy from the helicopter, it's pretty full.

Victor's face is already red from the sun. As he talks, it gets redder and redder. I like his mom a lot, but she does worry. It drives him crazy.

"I'm really tired, Ma. I spent the night at a girl's camp-site. What? I said a girl's campsite. Aw, Ma! It wasn't like that. I was under a canoe. I said a canoe. No, you can't do anything. A canoe – a boat. Yes, Ma. I'm fine. I'm warm enough, Ma. It's hot. I said I'm warm enough. How are you? Yes, I'm tired. Tired. Yes, a bit hungry too. No, I'm not starving. I had fish for dinner last night. Fish! What? I said fish, not wish. No, I don't wish I was with you, Ma. I want to stay. They're having a games day at the camp tomorrow, and they've invited me and Alan to play too."

The camp director is a jolly middle-aged woman about the size and shape of an elephant. She wears a hat that says CAMP DIRECTOR, in case you forget, and shorts that are wider than I am tall. She sounds like a foghorn – no wonder they call her Boomer. Right now she's beaming at Victor.

Dr. Callous is a skinny little guy with a stoop and a cig-arette, and tufts of dark hair sprouting from unexpected places – his ears and his nose and the top of his T-shirt. He's taking my temperature and pulse, and frowning.

"Yes, Alan's here too. He already called home. For the last time, I'm fine, Ma," says Victor. "All I want is a chance to rest. . . . Yes. I said yes. I do too. Oh, Ma, I can't say it now. People are here." He hangs up, the color of a ripe strawberry.

The doctor finishes with me and stands there, cigarette smoke rising and swirling, getting trapped in his nose hairs and eyebrow hairs. He has spider legs: long and skinny and covered in hair.

"Do they have to go to the hospital in Peterborough, doc?" asks the helicopter pilot. "'Cause if not, I've got to get back to Kawartha."

"I don't think so," says the doctor. "Nothing here that a day of rest won't cure. I'm a little concerned about this one." Meaning me. The doctor has a dry raspy voice, like sandpaper. He wears a pen on a string around his neck. He uses it to make a note on the clipboard he carries.

The pilot snorts. "Ah, him! The mouthy one."

"Hey!" I say. "What was that?"

"You heard me, kid."

– *Ru-di-pimp-ig!* says Norbert.

"Rudipimpig?" Dr. Callous is right beside me. "Is that what you said?"

"No," I say.

– *Yes*, says Norbert.

"That's what I mean. Boy's suffering from mild hypothermia." The doctor makes another note. "He's delirious."

"No, I'm not!"

Victor asks what hypothermia is.

"Low body temperature," says Dr. Callous. "Brought on by exposure."

"Do I have hypothermia?" asks Victor. The doctor shakes his head.

"Neither do I. I'm fine!" I say.

"Classic," says the doctor. "One of the symptoms of hypothermia is to claim that you feel fine when you don't."

"But I do feel fine," I say.

133

"See?" says the doctor. "There you go again."

"I feel kind of sick," says Victor. "I guess I must be okay, then."

They make us both lie down. Everyone but the doctor leaves. "Do you want to call home again?" Boomer asks me, on her way out. No one answered when I called the first time.

"No, thanks," I say. "I left a message on the machine. My mom knows I'm okay."

Next thing I know, it's lunchtime. Dr. Callous brings us our meals on trays. I eat every bite. A pathetic figure hobbles into the infirmary as I'm finishing. A middle-aged guy with thick dark hair, thick dark mustache. He has a crutch under one arm, and a nurse supporting the other. He sees us and smiles. Big white teeth.

"Boys!" he calls. "Great to see you! Just great! How are you?"

"Fine, Mr. Leech," says Victor.

"Just fine," I say.

"That's wonderful. Just wonderful. What a horrible night! I was real worried about you," says Christopher. He steps up to my bedside and offers me his right hand. I don't want to shake it, but I do.

"How are you feeling, Mr. Leech?" asks Victor.

"Thanks for asking, Vic. Not too bad. Got a sprained ankle, and some bruises. I've been recuperating since yesterday." He squeezes the nurse's arm. *Ew.* This man is hanging around my house, going out with my mom, and he's squeezing a nurse. She has dark hair and a tan.

"You boys should thank this man," says the doctor. "When he arrived here yesterday, he could hardly talk, but he insisted on immediate search and rescue helicopters. Maybe next time you go camping, you won't run away, hey?"

"*Why* did you tell everyone that?" I point my finger at Christopher. I've been meaning to ask him.

"What?"

"That we ran away. Why did you say it, when it isn't true? The helicopter pilot called us stupid kids. Everyone seems to think it's all our fault we got lost. Why did you tell them that? It *wasn't* our fault. It was your fault. *You* ran away. We saw you on the lake, paddling away from us."

He sighs. His eyebrows and his mustache go down. "Now, son –"

"I'm not your son."

"Well, then. As a matter of fact, you're wrong. You did run away. I was on the portage with you, and then you wandered off."

"And what happened to you?"

"I looked for you."

"And then? What happened to you then? *Why did you leave?*"

The doctor clears his throat. "Maybe you two should get some sleep. You especially, Alan. Do you want another blanket?"

"I'm fine," I say.

"Fine? You're still fine?" Dr. Callous shakes his head. "That hypothermia . . . dear, dear."

Christopher is already at the door. "I'll look in again later," he says. "Say, um, did you call your mom?" He's so casual. I nod. "Good. Good." He looks hard at me. "Good," he says again, and takes the nurse's arm on his way out the door.

Strangely enough, I don't feel wholly angry. A large part of me feels relieved. We're saved, Victor and me. The grown-ups have taken charge. They may not believe our story, but they're not going to bite us or maul us, or let us starve or freeze to death. The worst is over.

Mind you, I'm still mad. It is *not* our fault we got lost. Christopher left us. I wonder why? And there's one other thing on my mind, one other tangle in the knot I'm trying to unravel.

"Hey, Vic," I whisper. "What do you think happened to the artist lady?"

No sound from the other bed. The covers rise and fall regularly.

When I wake up again, it's much later. The setting sun throws long shadows across the floor of the infirmary. Dust specks float gently down. I lie in bed, thinking about the artist lady and her kayak. Thinking about Christopher and the nurse, and Mom. The infirmary has unpainted wooden walls and posters of needles and one of those big charts showing if you are overweight for your height. My doctor's office has one of them too. I checked it a couple of years ago when I was bored, sitting in the small waiting room after sitting in the big waiting room. I matched my height and weight, following over and across, and concluded that the ideal height for my weight would be eight feet, three inches tall. This worried me, so I asked the doctor about it. She laughed and told me the lines were centimeters, not inches.

The door opens and a supermodel walks in. That's what she looks like. Taller than Dr. Callous, who's with her. She has long flowing blonde hair, a pert little nose, wide-set eyes, healthy tan, long legs. Her clothes are . . . well, they're perfect. Her camp sweater is knotted casually around her shoulders. Her shorts are just the right length. Her camp T-shirt looks as if it just came back from the dry cleaner.

She stares at me for a long ten seconds. I feel like a painting on a wall – not a very good painting. She stares at Victor too, then turns to the doctor. "Which one is Alan?" she asks.

I sit up, clear my throat.

"This one," says the doctor. He's taking my temperature.

"Hi," I say.

She doesn't reply. "He's the troublemaker, right?"

"Yes," says the doctor.

"Hey!" I say.

"You see?" says the doctor.

The supermodel nods. "What's wrong with his nose?"

I swallow. Does she know about Norbert?

"Sunburn," says the doctor. "Nothing serious."

The supermodel comes closer to my bed. She's so *healthy*. The skin on her arm and hand is smooth and warm and glowing, and totally without flaw. No moles, freckles, beauty spots. No cuts or bruises. I can't help thinking of Zinta's big dirty capable fingers.

"Will they be able to compete tomorrow, doc?" she asks. "They don't look like much."

"I think so, Trixie," the doctor rasps. "They're better than they were this morning. Alan's temperature is normal."

Trixie. Where do I know that name from? She turns to me.

"How long would it take you to split a cord of wood, Alan?"

I clear my throat. "What's a cord of wood?"

"Can you start a one-match fire?"

I shake my head. I don't even know what she's talking about.

"Could you paddle across the lake, portage a canoe a hundred yards, and paddle back?"

I shake my head.

"What *can* you do?"

– *Hey! You remind me a lot of Nerissa*, says Norbert.

Why does he choose moments like this to enter the conversation? Nerissa is his girlfriend, back on Jupiter. Quite a tough cookie, apparently, but he really likes her.

Trixie doesn't notice because she's frowning at the doctor, who has a cigarette in his mouth. "Do you mind?" she snaps.

"Oh, sorry," he says, and puts the cigarette in his pocket.

Wow. I try to imagine my doctor hurrying to do something because I asked him to. Can't do it. I can't imagine any grown-up hurrying to do what I asked them to. In fact, now that I'm on the topic, I can't imagine *anyone* – anyone at all, from my own doctor ("Two and a half centimeters to the inch, Alan. Oh, ho ho!") to colorful Uncle Emil to little Mary Lee Noscowitz, who lives down the street and rides her tricycle past our house – hurrying to do my bidding. I'm just not the sort of guy people obey. Mind you, I don't look like a supermodel.

She frowns at me. "You're no good at anything, are you?"

– *She says stuff like this all the time.*

"Who are you talking about?"

– *Nerissa, of course. Haven't you been listening?*

The girl leans down. "It's like this, Alan. I'm the captain of the Trailblazer team for games day tomorrow. One of my team sprained his ankle yesterday, and won't be able to play, so old Boomer said we could ask you guys to take his place."

"Uh-huh," I say.

"But you're no good to me, Alan. No good at all. Is your friend any better? He looks stronger than you. Has he ever been camping?"

I nod. I've got her placed now. Trixie Mintworthy. Zinta's archenemy. I can believe it.

139

– You make me homesick. Of course Nerissa is prettier than you are. But that's not your fault. You can't help the way you look.

She jerks her head up. Bit of a pout now. Still looks like a supermodel, though – they often get photographed with pouts. "What's wrong with the way I look?" she asks.

I open my mouth to say "nothing," but Norbert gets in there first.

– You have too many arms, he says.

She stares at me. "I want Victor on my team," she says. "This weirdo can join the Lumberjacks." At which point, Zinta knocks and comes in.

The girls are instantly aware of each other. Trixie stands away from me and the doctor, as if readying herself for combat. Zinta's eyes widen. The girls circle cautiously. They're like animals. If they had fur, it would be standing up. I can almost feel them growing physically larger, more threatening.

The doctor's cell phone rings. He takes it out of his pocket.

"Well, if it isn't the Master Tripper," says Trixie. Her voice drips scorn. "Fresh from her night in the wilderness. Too bad you didn't get a chance to wash your hair." She smooths her own hair – not that it needs it.

Zinta narrows her eyes. "You should try a night in the wilderness, Trixie. Of course, you'd have to be able to run the rapids without smashing your canoe."

"Very amusing, Zinta. Very droll. Yes, you certainly earned your scroll. Hope you enjoy it – while you have it."

Zinta's face fills with blood.

Trixie gives a tinkling laugh. "Yes, that scroll is going to look good on my trophy shelf. When your mom saves up enough food stamps, maybe you'll get a shelf for your trophies too."

"You leave my mom out of this, or I'll –"

Trixie puts her hand to her mouth. "Oh, my! Must watch that temper of ours. Doctor, should Zinta be here? We wouldn't want her losing control and hurting these two little boys."

The doctor is still on the phone. "I'll be right down to the heliport," he says. "Try the hospital in Peterborough." He hurries out of the cabin.

Zinta isn't talking, but her look is so full of menace, so frightening that I want to pull the covers up over my head. And she's not even looking at me.

Trixie's expression is pretty frightening too. Bully frightening. She's a mean one. "It's going to be a pleasure to get that scroll away from you tomorrow," she says.

"You think you will win?" Zinta clenches her hands into fists. Veins stand out in high relief on her bicep and tricep muscles. "We're going to take you. I know it."

"You're bluffing, Zinta. Remember last year's game? I can always tell when you're bluffing. Oh, and speaking of games, I get what's-his-name tomorrow. Him." She points.

"Victor?"

"Yes, Victor is a Trailblazer. He's going to replace Billy from the Weasel cabin. If you want, you can have this weird guy here."

That would be me.

Trixie stares at me. "Not enough arms," she says, shaking her head. I don't say anything. Trixie spins on her heel and walks out the door.

"I hate that girl," says Zinta.

19

I Am Dougal

"It'll be dinner soon," says Zinta. "Boomer sent me to ask if you and Victor could eat with us in the dining hall."

"Sure," I say. "Sounds good."

"Do you think Dr. Callous would let you? I heard something about hypothermia."

"I'm fine!" I say. "No one seems to believe me, but I'm fine. I can even play in these games of yours."

"The games. The games." She starts to pace back and forth. "Trust Trixie to get here first," she mutters. "At least Victor is a camper. What can *you* do?" She whirls around. "Sorry, Alan. I didn't mean to say that out loud."

"That's okay. I've . . . um . . . been thinking about how I can help you. And I've come up with a way."

"How?"

A bell rings somewhere in the distance. A warning? A symbol? We'll see. "I'll beat Trixie at poker for you," I say.

She stops pacing. Her eyebrows go up. "How can you do that? I know you beat me last night, in the tent, but that was luck, right? Poker's all luck, isn't it?"

"Do you know what I'm thinking?" I say.

She shakes her head.

"Well, a lot of poker is knowing what the other guy is thinking. And, for some reason, I seem to be good at that. I'm no good at tying knots and carrying canoes and starting fires. But I can tell what you're thinking right now."

"You can?"

I stare into her eyes and nod solemnly.

It takes a moment for her to accept this. I don't change my expression.

She nods a couple of times. "Gee, Alan! That's great!" She smiles.

I let myself relax, return her smile.

"Hey, you're good," she says. "Maybe you *can* help us."

– *He's bluffing.*

"Quiet, Norbert."

– *He has no idea what you're thinking.*

Now Zinta's face clouds over. "Wh-at? What did you say, Alan?"

"Nothing."

"Were you bluffing, just now? Do you know what I'm thinking?"

The bell keeps tolling, loud and deep. Victor stirs and wakes up.

"How're you feeling?" I ask him.

"Hungry." He rubs his stomach. He's missing a few potato chips since yesterday.

"Good timing," Zinta tells him. "That's the summoning bell. Dinner is in fifteen minutes."

Camp Omega (OUTDOOR EXPERIENCE SINCE 1910! says the sign outside the infirmary) is laid out on rocks and under trees. Zinta takes us on a quick tour before dinner. There are paths everywhere, lined with woodchips. We pass cabins with animal names: Chipmunk, Raven, Weasel. Each one seems to have a droopy clothesline strung between trees, with soggy towels and bathing suits hanging down. The Weasel cabin is hung with a banner saying TRAILBLAZERS.

"That's your team, Victor," I tell him. "You're a Trailblazer."

"Huh?"

"Camp games day is tomorrow. You're on Trixie's team."

"Who's Trixie?"

"You'll find out."

We pass a cabin with a LUMBERJACK banner. "I'm a Lumberjack," I say.

"And I'm a Trailblazer? Okay, I get it. My camp had a games day too: Iroquois and Blackfoot. I was a Blackfoot. My cabin won the Red Rover competition."

Zinta nudges me. "How did you do in Red Rover, Alan?" she whispers.

"I don't think I've ever played Red Rover," I say.

Zinta looks grave.

"Hey, Zinta!" calls a little kid with a LUMBERJACK T-shirt. "We're going to get 'em tomorrow!"

"You better believe it, Rocky!" she says.

A couple of other little kids are coming down another path. "Lumberjacks – hah!" they shout. "Trailblazers! Trailblazers!"

Zinta smiles.

We pass the infirmary again on our way to the top of a hill, and come to a building with different animals carved in wood outside it. Kids and grown-ups are lining up to go in. "Dining hall," says Zinta. "It'll turn into a casino tomorrow night."

She gives me a meaningful glance. I give her the thumbs-up.

It's getting chilly, as the sun sinks towards the hills. I wish I had a change of clothes.

"Well, hello there! Glad to see you on your feet!" It's Boomer, jiggling like a pudding. Her CAMP DIRECTOR button flashes in the sunlight. She shakes hands with Victor and then, after a pause, with me. Zinta disappears.

"No time to stop," says Boomer, striding off. "Another helicopter just came in. Find yourselves places to sit in the hall," she calls over her shoulder.

Victor and I stare at each other. Shrug.

"I can smell something cooking," I say. "What is it?"

His nose is better than mine – sorry, Norbert, I didn't mean that. His sense of smell is better.

"Salisbury steak," he says. "With barbecue sauce!"

We join the line of kids on their way to dinner.

The dining hall is a long thin rectangle. Tables set down a long center aisle. Over each table, hanging from the ceiling, is a large and lifelike wooden sculpture of an animal. Each cabin sits at its own table.

It's a busy, noisy place. Benches clatter. Shouts echo off the cement floor. People move quickly to their places.

I cannot help but notice that there is a division among the animals. Looking down the right-hand side, from where I stand, are a dove, a beaver, a chipmunk, and an owl. Wise and hardworking animals, portrayed in white or cream colored woods. Their feathers and fur are all in place, neat and groomed. They appear to be smiling. The forces of light.

Down the left-hand side, the animals are carved out of darker wood. They're not carved as well, either. There are scratches and cuts, and some of the animals have a decidedly scruffy appearance. And they're different animals too: foxes, ravens, weasels, and snakes. These animals frown, glower, sneer. The wood is older, and, in the case of the snake, stained and blotched. This is the dark side.

Victor and I stand at the front of the hall. We don't have a place to go. Everyone stares at us. I feel their eyes. They're checking us out, commenting. Do we pass? I'm very aware of my sunburnt nose.

Christopher and his nurse sit at the head table, with the other grown-ups. She has her hand on his arm. He smiles past her, searching the room. I look away before he gets to me.

"Who's that?" Victor is staring at the Snake table. "That girl with the blonde hair is staring at me."

"That's Trixie," I mutter.

"She's still looking. Do you think she wants me to sit with her? Me?" He points to himself. Trixie nods, and beckons.

"Wow!" he says.

Oh, Victor. Oh, my friend. "Be careful," I caution, but it's too late. He's gone.

The atmosphere is boisterous, but also orderly and attentive. The dining hall is obviously an important place in the life of the camp. A meeting place, a place of order, ritual, duty, veneration. In its way, a holy place. I don't belong. I'm reminded of Dougal, who joined our grade four class in midterm. His mom was doing a teaching exchange of some kind. Dougal was our age, and size, but he wore short pants and striped socks, and spoke with a broad Scottish accent. And he couldn't skate – something as natural as breathing to us. As far as we were concerned, he might have been a different species. He went home at the end of the year, but we still talk about him. The strange Scottish kid.

Oh, no. I am Dougal. I wonder if they'll talk about me in three years.

"Over here, Alan," calls Zinta. At last! Someone wants me. I walk over. Needless to say, Zinta's table is on the other side of the hall from Trixie's. The light side. She's under the sculpture of the owl. It's all girls at the Owl table. "Sit with the Beavers," Zinta tells me, pointing at the table next to her.

I find a spot on the Beaver bench. "Hi, there," I say. No one replies. Maybe if I try an accent. "*Wheesht*, lads, but it's a braw nicht the nicht!" Dougal, wherever you are, I apologize for the way I treated you in fourth grade.

Boomer strides in at this point and squats in front of an amplifier, fiddling with a wire. From the back she looks enormous: a new continent or something. I feel like I should plant a flag in her and claim her for Canada.

You know, that's a pretty funny idea. I want to share it with someone. I turn to the guy beside me, but he's looking solemn right now. So's everyone else around the table. Come to think of it, the whole dining hall is quiet and respectful.

Boomer is on her feet. "Campers and guests!" She doesn't need her microphone. Her voice bounces all over the big room. "Let us say our grace!"

We all rise together, Lumberjack and Trailblazer, light and dark, good and evil. We bow our heads as Boomer recites a prayer:

> For the food we eat
> For the friends we greet
> For the day so sweet.
> Thank you.

That's all. You know, I don't think it's funny. In fact, it sounds pretty good. I say amen, with everyone else.

20

Um to Me

The kid next to me is staring. "Your nose must hurt, Alan," he says, with his mouth full. He's a tough kid, like a length of rawhide. Looks like he can tie himself in knots. Mike? Is that his name? Mark, maybe? Something like that. Zinta introduced me around the two tables, but I can't remember any of the names.

"I beg your pardon?" I say.

"It's all red. Your cheeks and forehead too, but your nose is really red. You got a bad sunburn." The kid talks around a plug of food in his cheek. Without swallowing, he takes a bite of Salisbury steak and keeps chewing. His jaw muscles bulge. He adds a forkful of mashed potatoes to the bite and keeps chewing. Then a bite of canned carrots and peas. Then another bite of steak. He's a conveyor belt, never stopping. He grabs the plate of bread, takes a piece, and offers the plate to me. "Bread, Alan?"

"No, um . . . ," I say. *Um.* Good name for him.

"I'll take a piece of bread. Thanks, Peter," says the redhead on the other side of me. Drat! I thought *he* was Peter. Maybe he's Mike. Or Mark.

Peter, the skinny tough kid, takes a slice and slathers some margarine on it. Peter. Peter. The counselor at the Beaver table is the one with the bangs and the sharp jutting chin – I met her this morning at the campsite. Her name is Belinda. I think. The two boys across from me are Derek and Eric. One of them is dark skinned, and one light skinned, but I forget which is which. They're both wearing striped shirts.

Oh, the heck with it. Maybe they'll all go on being *Um* to me.

Is my nose red? I reach up and feel my nose furtively. A bit warm, I suppose.

– *HEY!* shouts Norbert.

The table stops to stare at me. Peter has his fork halfway to his mouth.

"It's the sunburn talking," I say.

"Hello, Omega campers!" booms Boomer.

No microphone. We're outside, all of us, sitting on tree trunk benches around a roaring campfire. Twilight. Sun behind the hills. Crickets in the grass. It's almost bedtime. This is the official kickoff for the games.

I'm with the rest of the Lumberjacks. We're all fizzing with excitement, bubbling and buzzing and whispering. On the other side of the campfire, the Trailblazers grumble and mutter to each other.

"A couple of announcements," booms Boomer. "Could I have Zinta Zeeler here please."

Cheers from our side of the fire. Hoots and whistles from the other side.

Blushing all the way down to her neckline, Zinta drags her feet up beside the camp director. Boomer grabs her by the elbow, turns her around to face the crowd.

"You all know Zinta. She's been a camper here for years. She's the captain of the Lumberjack team. Yesterday, Zinta passed some really tough canoeing tests, including running the Bearclaw Rapids on the other side of Alpha Lake. (Cheers from all around the fire.) Then she stayed overnight without supervision, clearing her camp-site, pitching her tent and lighting her fire, catching her dinner, and staying dry despite a tremendous storm! (Cheers!) Zinta, it is my very great pleasure to present you with this Master Tripper Scroll." (Extra loud cheers!)

I expect the scroll to be something mystical and ancient – the sort of thing Harry Potter would get if he went canoeing. It looks like a plain piece of paper, with string tied around the middle.

"And that's not all," Boomer goes on. "Yesterday, Zinta did something more important than winning the Master Tripper Scroll. Would Victor and Alan come up here, please?"

Victor is sitting beside Trixie. When he stands up, I happen to notice the expression on her face. Never have I seen such intense hatred coming from one person, and I include Big Mary, the nastiest of the bullies back at my school in Cobourg. Maybe it's because Mary – fat as a banker's wallet, mean as a dentist's drill, strong as a steer roper – hates everyone, and Trixie hates one person. Very focused hatred.

Trixie hates Zinta. As much as Zinta hates her, she hates Zinta more.

Boomer explains about Zinta finding us wandering in the wilderness, and feeding and giving us shelter, and maybe saving our lives. She calls Christopher Leech's name. He's at the back of the crowd. He stands up and waves. Zinta blushes and looks away. We blush and look stupid. The campers cheer and whistle. "Hey, we helped too," Victor whispers in my ear. "What about my safety pin?"

The nurse helps Christopher to sit down. He looks around the campfire as he's smiling at the nurse, and I realize that I do not like him at all.

I think about all the hatred in the room right now – Trixie and Zinta, and me. And I can feel my Salisbury steak moving around in my stomach.

Boomer has a hand on my shoulder. Her fingers are the size of bananas. "For those of you who don't know, Victor and Alan will be competing in the games tomorrow," she announces. "Victor is an honorary Trailblazer, and Alan is an honorary Lumberjack. I understand that Victor has some camping experience. Isn't that right?" And she turns and smiles at Victor. It occurs to me that my friend *looks* like he's had camping experience. It's all the pockets in his clothes. Everything he's wearing – shorts, of course, but shirt too, and hat, and underpants for all I know – has pockets. Camping seems to require a lot of things, and the prepared camper has places to put them.

Now Victor reaches deep into a side pocket and pulls out a yellow rag. He waves it over his head. There's a murmur, and some whistling, from the assembled weasels and skunks and porcupines on their side of the campfire. I guess the yellow rag means something.

Boomer smiles and turns to me. "And Alan, here, is . . ." and then she stops. I am very aware of my unbuttoned shirt, oversized bathing shorts, and sunburnt face. "Well, we're happy to have him anyway," she says.

No cheers or whistles. I can hear the crickets very clearly. Ah, well.

Boomer waves the two of us back to our seats.

"Okay, campers. Let's see if we can predict a winner of the games. Are you ready? Are you ready to cheer for your team?" We cheer.

"That's it? That's as loud as you can cheer?"

We cheer louder.

"Not bad," says Boomer. "But I'll bet you can do better. Watch carefully now, Lumberjacks!"

A new fire blazes into sudden life off to the side of the field. Two large pieces of wood have been put together to make a capital letter *L*, and then set alight. The people around me start to cheer the burning *L*. *L* for Lumberjacks, I guess. I join in.

"Now it's your turn, Trailblazers!" The other side of the campfire is silent until another outsized letter leaps into startling flame on the other side of the field. A letter *T*. The Trailblazers cheer. We keep cheering. The fiery letters burn.

"Are you ready for tomorrow, campers?" calls Boomer. "I want you to show me how ready you are. Lumberjacks, Trailblazers, PUT ON YOUR UNIFORMS!"

Huh? A confused squirming lasts only a few seconds, and then everyone is on their feet, wearing a new T-shirt. The Trailblazers' shirts are yellow. The team name is written in black script across the front. The Lumberjacks around me are wearing – I have to check because it's getting dark – green shirts, with white lettering.

Victor's got a Trailblazer shirt. That was the yellow rag he was waving a minute ago.

I lean towards my neighbor. He's still cheering the letter *L*. "Nice shirt, Mike," I shout. "Do I get one too?"

"My name isn't Mike," he shouts.

"Mark?" I try, but he's turned away. Ah, well.

Boomer's voice booms even louder. "Get to bed everyone. Get lots of sleep. Tomorrow . . . LET THE GAMES BEGIN!"

We keep cheering as we leave the field and walk back to the cabins. The *T* goes out. The *L* teeters and falls. We keep cheering. I feel false, like I'm playing a part, but I cheer along with everyone else. When I get back to the infirmary, there's someone sleeping in my bed.

Not *in* my bed. On it, with a whole pile of comforters on top. There's a bag of clear stuff hanging on a metal pole beside the bed, dripping into the patient. The room lights are low. Dr. Callous is bending over the patient, shining a flashlight into her eyes. She moans faintly. I know who it is, of course. Not from her voice, which is even raspier than the doctor's, or her face, which is scrunched away from the light. Her glasses are gone, and the braid has come out of her hair, but I would recognize her feet anywhere. They stick up like a mountain range beneath the comforters. No one else in the world has feet like that.

"Hi, there . . . um, Doris," I say.

She moans some more.

"Is she going to be all right?" asks Victor.

The doctor stands away from the bed. "I still can't get much of a response," he says. "You kids had better stay out of the way until the ambulance comes."

Poor Doris. I feel terrible. It's our fault she's in this mess.

"I wish there was something we could do," I say.

"She was out in her kayak all night," says the doctor. "The rangers found her washed up at the far end of the lake." He shakes his head. "Say, how do you boys know her?"

"We saw her in her kayak," I say.

"We've been to her cabin," says Victor.

– *The cabin with the brilliant painting on the wall*, says Norbert. *When I saw it, I was transplanted! Too bad Orion was a bit out of drawing.*

Doris moves a little in the bed. She shakes her head. "Drawing," she mutters. "Out of drawing!"

"What's that?" The doctor moves quickly back to her side. "You seem to have woken her up. Hello, Miss Appel. Hello. It's Dr. Callous. Hello. Can you hear me?"

– *He sounds like he's talking on the telephone*, says Norbert.

"Is she going to be okay?" asks Victor.

– *Yes.*

"How do you know, Alan?"

"I don't."

– *I do. She'll be fine in a few days.*

The doctor bends low to ask Doris some questions. She replies weakly. He shakes his head, and keeps talking.

"Why transplanted, Norbert?" I ask. "Don't you mean you were transported?"

Mom uses that kind of word all the time. Last week she told me she was transported back to her youth on the wings of a radio song. The song was called "In-A-Gadda-Da-Vida," and midway through an extended drum solo, I was transported upstairs to watch TV.

– *Transplanted. As if I was back in my own garden. Jupiter never looked so blue. It made me homesick.*

When the ambulance comes, Doris is sitting up in her bed. The doctor tells the ambulance guys to be careful, and to keep her warm. "She got caught in the storm yesterday. Dropped her paddle in the middle of the lake, and couldn't make it to shore."

The ambulance guys strap her onto a flat movable bed. "Hypothermia?" asks the one with the clipboard.

The doctor raises his eyebrows. "She *says* she's fine."

They shake their heads sadly. They know what that means.

Ten minutes later I'm in bed. "Wonder what happened to her cabin?" I murmur. Victor is snoring. Norbert doesn't answer. I go to sleep.

21

Guess Who?

The games start right after breakfast, and go on all day. Is it the longest day of my life? No, of course not. Earlier this summer, surrounded by strangers in the middle of a scary big city, I spent an entire day waiting for my father to call me – and that seemed to go on forever. Once when I was six, I spent most of an afternoon waiting for the dentist to get to me and that was pretty awful, and then he did get to me, and that was even worse. But this late August day at Camp Omega seems to last a pretty darn long time. So many games I cannot play well. So much confusion. So many people shouting and trying hard.

It's like an all-you-can-eat buffet in a liver 'n onions restaurant. It's crowded and busy, and I don't want to eat anything. Not even the ice cream.

Some bad moments early on. Not highlights – low lights, maybe. The tug-of-war, for instance. What a disaster! Guess who stumbles and falls forward, tripping the person in front of him, who in turn trips the person in front of her, who trips the one in front of her, and so on, so that the whole Lumberjack team goes down like a row of dominoes, cursing the person on the end who started it? Guess who that person is? Right.

Guess who has to gunwale bob? ("It's easy!" Zinta whispers. "If you can walk, you can gunwale bob!") Guess who finds out that gunwale bobbing means balancing precariously on one end of the canoe while a fiendish laughing opponent in a yellow shirt jumps up and down on the other end, trying to bounce and knock you off? Go on, guess. Right again. I don't see Zinta when I fall out of my own canoe in the shallow water, much to the delight of the yellow-shirted team.

"Good try, Alan," the Lumberjacks say, smiling bravely and wishing me dead.

"Sorry," I say. "Sorry, Derek," or "Sorry, Mike."

Is there a height of humiliation? Maybe the war canoe race, where ten of us are paddling hard, but only one of us misses the water, bangs his paddle against the paddler behind him, turns to apologize, and falls out of the boat.

Guess who?

Hearing the cheers when Victor takes his turn at Red Rover is pretty tough, too. Our group of Lumberjacks from the Dove and Beaver cabins stands in the middle of the field, arms linked, like an impregnable wall.

Victor charges like a bull, right at me. He runs through my hands. His team of Trailblazers cheers. I think they're mostly from the Fox cabin. We call him again. He runs through me again, barreling up to my place in the chain and knocking my hands away from Eric or Derek, or whoever it is. We can't stop him. Correction: I can't stop him.

His team cheers. I can't hate him, but I wish him somewhere else.

We stop the rest of the Foxes. It helps that Zinta is with us for this game. We could have used her for the tug-of-war. Trixie stops by to watch the progress of her Trailblazers. "COME ON!" she shouts. "You can get past these little Doves!"

Zinta has a glint in her eye. "Red Rover, Red Rover," she cries, "we call *Trixie* over!"

Trixie stares at Zinta, then away. Then at Zinta again. She starts off for my end of the line, but veers away from me. She can't help herself. Zinta is a magnet for her. It's as if she's running unconsciously. She ends up hitting Zinta at full speed – eyes wide, mouth open, teeth bared, blonde hair streaming. What a mistake. Zinta stands straight and tall, and does not budge. Trixie bounces right off her like a soccer ball off a goalpost. She lies on the ground for a second, stunned.

"Change over," calls the referee, a no-nonsense counselor in black and white.

Trixie gets up, breathing heavily. "You wait, Zinta!" she says in a husky voice. "I am going to annihilate you!"

Then she stomps away. Our team does not taunt her. We're too nice.

All of us except Norbert.

– *You've got mud in your hair,* he calls.

She whirls around. "Who said that?" she hisses.

"Come on, come on, change over!" The referee looks at her watch.

Trixie doesn't move. "Who said I had mud in my hair?"

My team looks at me. "Um, actually," I say.

– *All down the back,* says Norbert. *A dark brown streak. Like a horse's mane. Very interesting.*

"Are you calling me a *horse*?" snaps Trixie.

– *With a brown mane,* says Norbert. *A lovely color. On Jupiter, brown is the color of hope.*

"Red Rover, Red Rover, we call . . ." They pause. Victor whispers. "Alan," they cry. "We call Alan over."

"Come and get it, loser!" calls Trixie.

"Now see what you've got me into, Norbert," I mutter.

I figure if I run slowly, I won't hurt myself as much. I angle myself towards Victor. I don't want any surprises. I'm nearly there, jogging along comfortably, trying to pick a place on the field to land, when I feel a tingle in my nose.

– *Looky, looky!* cries Norbert. *Over there, by the cabin. Skinny-dippers!!*

22

A Guy Like Alan

Of course there aren't any skinny-dippers. There isn't even a lake. We're playing on the field behind the dining hall, where we had the campfire last night. But there's something about the idea of skinny-dippers. The entire Trailblazer line turns to stare. Their arms get twisted, and they fall over each other, and I run through easily.

– *Heu heu heu!* Norbert gives his high-pitched, squeaky laugh. *Brown hair, brown shoes, we win, you lose!*

This is hard to resist. I laugh out loud before I can stop myself. Eric and Derek giggle, and repeat it to each other.

Trixie gets so mad she jumps up, runs after me, and pushes me down in the mud. The referee calls a bad sportsmanship penalty, and we win the game.

Things get a bit better after that. My teammates stop treating me like Leroy the Leper. They even laugh at a few of my jokes. At dinner, kids from the other Lumberjack tables come over to say hi.

"Did you really call Trixie a horse?" asks one of the Chipmunks.

"Well, no," I say.

"Because she does kind of look like one. She's a model, you know, but she has this long horsey face. A good-looking horse, mind you."

Victor sidles over just before dessert. "Trixie is really mad at you," he whispers. "She says it's all because of you that we lost the Red Rover game."

"Oh," I say.

From my side of the dining hall I hear a chorus of giggling voices. "Brown hair, brown shoes, we win, you lose!"

Victor shakes his head. "She is really mad about that rhyme too," he says, sidling away. "Just thought I'd warn you."

"Here's your pudding, Alan," says one of the girls from the Owl cabin. She passes me a bowl.

"Thanks, um," I say.

Zinta checks her clipboard again and again. "I've added up the scores three times, and it's even worse than last year," she reports in a low voice. "I'm pretty sure Trixie's ahead right now. We *have* to win the casino night." She looks at me. "We have to!" she says.

I nod.

I'm sitting across the table from her. She stands up, grabs me by the shoulders and shakes me. "What am I thinking?" she says. "Come on, Alan, what am I thinking right now? You say you're good at this. You have to know, if you're going to win against Trixie."

I swallow. I don't know what to say. She's really upset.

– *I really like pudding*, says Norbert. *Especially chocolate pudding.*

Zinta drops her hands. "I wasn't thinking about pudding at all," she whispers.

There's a huge squeak of feedback from the microphone by the head table. Boomer thanks us for making this edition of the games a great success so far. She is looking forward to the casino night tonight.

"Right now the two teams are very close in total points," she says. "The Trailblazers (whistles and hoots from the dark side of the dining hall) won the log sawing competition, and the gunwale bobbing, and the tug-of-war. The Lumberjacks (cheers from the light side) won the swimming and the fire starting and the Red Rover. Lumberjacks would have won the war canoe race, only they were disqualified because there weren't enough paddlers in the canoe."

Laughter from both sides of the dining hall. I stare at my pudding.

"So," says Boomer, "the Trailblazers are slightly ahead. Bragging rights for this year will be decided in a few hours, over the spin of the roulette wheel, the roll of the dice, the bounce of the skee ball, and the turn of the cards." She wishes everyone good luck, and tells us all to leave so the staff can start to set up in the dining hall.

Christopher is sitting at the head table, beside the nurse. He hobbles over after dinner.

"So, how was your day?" he asks. "Did you have fun?"

"Well," I say.

"I have some bad news for you," he says. "I saw Dr. Callous this afternoon. It looks like we aren't going to be able to finish our canoe trip."

I hold open the door of the dining hall so he can hobble through.

"Stretched ligaments in my ankle," he says. "I'll have to stay off it for a few weeks."

Should I say I'm sorry about his injury? I still don't like him. "Oh, well," I say.

Sun's going down. There's a hint of chill in the air. I wish I had a coat. Leaves on the bushes nearby are starting to turn color. Spindly bushes, with fan-shaped leaves and fuzzy dark fruit. There are lots of them around. They seem able to cling to rocks.

"I talked to Victor earlier," says Christopher. "He said he didn't mind leaving early."

"Did you call Mom?" I ask.

He looks embarrassed. "As a matter of fact, I did," he says. "We had a long talk." He seems like he wants to say more, but can't decide how to put it. Then the nurse comes over.

"You should be elevating that ankle, Christopher," she says.

"Okay," he says.

"How does it feel?"

"Hurts," he says.

She clucks her tongue. "Oh, dear," she says. "I'll take you to see the doctor again."

Christopher hobbles away, with one hand on his crutch and the other on the nurse's arm. He winces and draws his breath in sharply.

"Oh, you poor thing!" she says.

My stomach lurches. My mom says that all the time.

Mike or Mark bounces up to me after supper. Big smile on his face. "Brown hair, brown shoes, we win, you lose!" he calls. "Got to say, I like that. Trixie nearly busted herself. What you doing now?"

I shrug. "Not much."

"Good. Zinta wants to see you in the Beaver cabin."

"Where is that?"

"Huh? Oh, that's right, you're staying in the infirmary. This way. I'll show you."

We head down the hill. He's an energetic guy. He runs ahead of me. The sun is setting right in my eyes. I squint, stumble, and barely regain my balance. Why should it bother me that the nurse reminds me of my mother? What does it mean?

The boys' cabin is dim and dank, and smells of wet clothes and dirty feet. There's room inside for three bunk beds, and a long bench running across the front, under the screened windows. Four people sit along the bench: Zinta, Eric and Derek, and Lex, a chubby guy who's the best swimmer in camp. Mike or Mark climbs into the middle upper bunk.

"Do you know skee ball, Alan?" asks Lex right away.

– *His bridle was silver*, sings Norbert. *His mane it was gold. And the worth of his saddle has never been told.*

Lex chuckles. "That's Stewball," he says. "Not skee ball."

"I don't know what skee ball is," I answer.

Zinta has her clipboard out. She makes a mark. "Count that as a no," she says.

There are, Zinta explains, four main games at casino night. Skee ball – and I know I'm getting ahead of myself again, but I'll say right now I never do find out how to play – roulette, dice, and poker. Each camper gets ten chips at the start of the night, and the team with more chips at the end wins. The Trailblazers won last year by saving all the chips they won at skee ball and dice and roulette, and giving them to their players at the poker table. Trixie was the big winner – she ended up with all the chips in play.

"Can you beat her, Alan?" asks Eric. He's the dark-skinned one. He's sweating more than the rest of us. "Zinta tells us you say you're pretty good. Are you?"

"Eric was in the poker final with me last year," says Zinta. "To get to the final, you have to clean out your first table."

There's a deck of cards on the bench. I pick it up, fan the cards out and back quickly, do a waterfall shuffle, and then cut the deck one-handed. I don't drop a single card.

"Pretty good!" says Derek. Mike or Mark gives a whistle of appreciation from the bunk.

I deal two hands. Why am I doing this at all? Why bother? Why risk the extra humiliation? I've had plenty already today.

Partly it's gratitude. I want to help Zinta, to pay her back for helping Victor and me. But it's pride too. I want to show them I'm good. I'm sick of being the guy who can't do anything.

The cards sit on the bench in two piles. Five cards each. "Okay, Eric," I say. "Let's play, you and me. Straight poker, no draw. Pretend you have a stack of chips. Would you bet this hand?"

He picks up his cards, studies them intently. "No."

"I bet two pretend chips," I say.

He cocks his head. "You didn't look at your hand."

"I don't have to. I was looking in your eyes. I know you don't like your hand. So my hand is bound to be better."

"Oh, yeah? Well, I'll see your pretend two chips, and raise two more."

"But, Eric, why would you do that? You're bluffing, trying to scare me. You want me to think you have good cards. But I know you don't like them. What's the point in bluffing if the other guy knows? I see your two chips and raise twenty."

His mouth opens. He checks his hand again. "I . . ."

"Do you want to put out twenty chips for a hand you don't like? Twenty chips is a lot. Does it make sense to bet a lot on a hand we both know is lousy? Come on, Eric."

"I . . ." He turns over his hand. "I fold."

"Yes. That's the right thing to do."

He smiles. "It is, isn't it."

I sit back. Zinta stares at Eric, then turns to me. "But . . . but, Alan, you won without even looking at your hand. How did you do that?"

I wink at her.

"Hey!" says Lex. "This guy's good!" He pats Eric on the back. "Too bad, Eric. Beat by a guy who didn't even pick up his cards." He holds up a hand for me to slap. "Hey, we might win after all. Wouldn't that be a kick in the pants for Trixie, if a guy like Alan can beat her."

What does he mean by "a guy like Alan"? What's wrong with being a guy like Alan?

– *Oh, Skeeball was a racehorse*, sings Norbert. *And I wish he were mine. He never drank water. He always drank* –

The bell from the dining hall rings.

"Show time," says Zinta.

23

I Want Her Down

The campers are milling around. Colored lights around the door spell out OMEGA CASINO. Victor pulls me away from the crowd. His TRAILBLAZERS T-shirt is too small for him. "I want to warn you about Trixie." He looks over his shoulder.

"What about her?"

"She really has it in for you, after this afternoon. I told her you played poker, and –"

"Hello, boys!" Boomer's chins wiggle. "Are you having fun, Victor? Alan, how's that hypothermia?"

I've learned my lesson. "I'm feeling a bit low," I say.

"That's the spirit! Enjoy casino night." She wanders away, slapping backs as she goes.

"What about Trixie?" I say.

"Yes, what about me?"

I stand away from Victor and look up. It's her, all right. Tall, slim, washed, and changed. Her hair is away from her forehead, pulled back in a no-nonsense ponytail. She pushes Victor out of the way and stares down at me.

"What did Victor say about me?"

She towers over me. I'm glad she's Zinta's problem, not mine. I wonder how good a poker player she is. I can't think of anything to say now. I don't want to get Victor in trouble.

– He said he saw bottles of horse liniment in your cabin.

Victor sputters. "Alan! Listen, uh, Trixie, I did not say that. I . . ."

"Would you leave us alone for a second, Victor?" she says. "Maybe pick up your chips and get over to the roulette wheel. I want to talk to Alan about six things."

"Huh? Oh, sure." He smiles nervously, and goes.

Trixie puts her arm on my shoulders and leads me around the side of the dining hall. We're out of sight now.

"You're a funny guy, Alan," she says. "Brown hair, brown shoes, ha ha ha. And Victor tells me you're a good card player. But you won't win tonight."

Her eyes jump around in her head. Her chin sticks out. "That's one thing I wanted to talk to you about. Here's five more." She waggles the fingers of her left hand in front of my face. She clenches them into a fist, and punches me in the nose with it. Then she spins on her heel, and walks away.

I am in shock. There's a ringing in my ears, but it's not the bell from the dining hall.

– *Earthquake!* shouts Norbert.

"Are you okay, Norbert?" I feel my nose. Doesn't seem to be broken. It hurts, though.

– *Something spilled here in the back room.*

"Blood?"

– *I think it might be cocoa,* says Norbert. *I was sitting in my easy chair, and now my mug of cocoa is gone. What happened? The lights flickered and I ended up on the carpet.*

"She punched . . . you," I say.

– *Punched? She punched me? That tall one?*

"Her. Trixie Mintworthy."

– *Punched me? Like I was a pillow?*

"Uh . . . yeah."

– *So. It's war.*

He doesn't say anything else. I move around to the front of the dining hall.

Victor comes up to me with his eyes wide. "What happened?" he says.

"Trixie." I wipe my nose cautiously on my sleeve. "She's got a good left," I say.

"She's good at cards too. Did you know she went to Las Vegas for a week, to take lessons from a poker teacher?"

I swallow. Las Vegas? I've never played poker in a room that didn't have a furnace in it. Why am I doing this again? I do not want to let Zinta down, but I may be out of my depth here.

"And she's out to get you, Alan. I'm glad I'm not going to be at your poker table."

I wait in line to get my chips. The counselor giving them out has shiny hair and chewed nails. "You're Alan, right?" he says. "The new kid. Here you go." He hands over my stack of chips, and writes my name at the bottom of a typed list.

Four round tables are set up along the far wall of the dining hall. I sit at table one with three other players. There's a counselor in a green LUMBERJACK T-shirt to act as referee.

"Draw poker is simple," he explains. "You get five cards. You bet. You get a chance to improve your hand by discarding the cards you don't want and drawing new ones. If you don't like your hand, you fold. If you like it – or if you want to bluff the other guys – you bet some more. The other guys either fold, or bet along. Everyone who calls the last bet shows their hand. Best hand wins. Understand?"

We nod. "Good luck, everyone," calls the counselor. "And now, ante up!"

We all throw chips in the middle of the table. The cards are in front of me. I deal.

The evening is under way. All I have to do is win. All I have to do is be the best. No pressure. None at all.

Five cards facedown. I stare at the familiar blue-backed cardboard rectangles. Relax, I tell myself. Pretend you're in Victor's basement. I check my cards, keeping them close together. Two tens and some garbage. Not a good hand. I put it down. I never look more than once. The cards won't change. Anyway, I'm more interested in the other players. The guy on my right drops a card on the table, picks it up, and drops his whole hand. Clumsy. The girl across from me thumbs carefully through her cards, and puts two of them in a special place. I figure she has a nice pair, kings or aces. On my left is a kid wearing mirror shades. I'm not kidding: mirror sunglasses at a poker game! That's not cool; that's stupid.

Nobody bets before the draw. Everyone takes three cards. I don't look at mine. I watch the others' faces, especially the girl's. If she draws another king or ace to make three of a kind. . . . She's disappointed. She didn't improve. Good.

I check my hand. I didn't improve either. Still the pair of tens, and that's all. Oh, well.

Shades' turn to bet first. "Nine chips!" he says confidently.

That's his whole stake. All he's got left after the ante. Sounds like he's got a huge hand. A straight or flush. Maybe better. The girl hasn't looked up from her cards. She's a cautious player. She folds. Good. The clumsy guy puts his cards down quickly. Good.

"Nine chips to you, dealer," says Shades. "Unless you want to fold too." He sounds eager. If I don't call his bet, he wins.

This is such a gift, it's hard to keep a straight face. You

see, I know Shades has a terrible hand. I can see it reflected in his sunglasses. "I'll call your bluff," I say.

Shades gulps, turns over his cards. King high. No pairs.

I show my pair of tens. He's out of the game and I have more than doubled my stake.

"Hey," says the cautious girl. "I had a pair of kings. I would have beat you."

Would have. "You didn't bet," I say. "You have to bet, to win."

"Next deal," says the counselor.

"How did you know I was bluffing?" Shades asks me.

"Let's say that I had a vision," I tell him.

We keep playing. Cautious gets a couple of really good hands, and cleans poor Clumsy out. Just two of us now. I bet five chips, and Cautious thinks I'm bluffing. She screws up her courage and throws in ten chips to scare me out. I raise her ten more. She uses her last chips to call with two pair – a pretty good hand. But I'm not bluffing this time. Two pair loses to three of a kind, and I have three sixes. I stand up from the table with forty chips.

"The poker final starts at eight o'clock," says the counselor. "You've got a half hour."

It's getting pretty raucous over at Trixie's table. "Ha HA!" she calls, slapping her cards down. "Kings full of aces. Read 'em and weep, Four Eyes!" She grabs a pile of chips. A kid with glasses looks unhappy.

I check the other tables. At table two, Zinta has a stack of chips in front of her. So do Eric and Derek at table three. Lumberjacks are winning. Maybe I won't have to do it all myself. "I'll be outside," I say to my table's counselor.

"Don't you want to play dice or skee ball?" he asks.

"No."

The bathroom looks like one of the regular cabins, but the smell is different, even from the outside. And from the inside it's worse.

– *When are we going to beat her down?*

"Who?" I'm washing my hands. I stare at the bathroom mirror. My hair is sticking up. My checked shirt is rumpled. I wet my hair, but it doesn't stay down.

– *You know who, Dingwall. And you look a mess. Don't worry about it. Are we going to beat her down?*

"Trixie? No, of course not. She's bigger than I am."

– *So what are we going to do? We can't let her punch us!*

"We're going to take her poker chips away. Then the Lumberjacks will win the games, and Zinta will be happy."

– *I want to beat her down.*

"You mean beat her up."

– *No I don't. When I'm finished, I want her DOWN.*

I step out the bathroom door, and stop dead. Christopher's voice is coming through an open window next door. "I feel so bad!" he says. Not the way a patient normally says this. "I left those boys alone in the woods," he says.

"But why?" asks the nurse. "Why did you do that?"

I want to know the answer too. I run up to the cabin, crawl past a prickly shrub, and peek in the window.

24

All Black

A storage cabin. Crates of canned goods on shelves. Bare walls, board floor. Harsh overhead light. Christopher limps back and forth underneath the light.

"Why?" he says. "You want to know why, Bernice? I'll tell you why. It was the bears."

Oh. I almost say it aloud. Time to reconsider, perhaps. Can I forgive him for running from bears? I think so. I think so. After all, I ran from them too.

"They were after me, Bernice. Following me. Faster and faster. I didn't know what to do. I knew I should warn the boys. I wanted to . . . but I didn't. I dropped the food pack. I dropped everything except the canoe. I couldn't think of anything except getting away from those bears. I was . . . scared, that's why. Plain scared."

"Oh, poor you," says Bernice. She's over by the shelves, gazing up at him. It creeps me out when she talks like my mom. She even has her intonation.

"And I thought, if I could draw the bears away from the boys, they'd have a better chance," he says. "You see, I know what bears can do to people."

He stands there under the bare bulb, twisting his hands together. "I hate bears. Do you know how strong bears are? Do you know how sharp their claws are? I was on a canoe trip once, years ago, with my best friend, and a grizzly bear came into our campsite. He . . . I can't say any more. It's too painful." He hides his face in his hands.

Wait a minute. Something not quite right here. Drawing the bears away? Like he's running away for *our* sake? That doesn't sound right. He's too obvious. He wants her sympathy.

If this conversation were a poker game, I'd call his bluff.

She believes him. "Oh, there there," she says, going over to pat his shoulder. "You poor brave man." She keeps her hand there.

"You understand! I knew you would. Oh, Bernice!"

"Oh, Chris!"

He puts his arms around her and starts kissing her. She lets him. Then she starts kissing him back. He reaches up to turn out the light. I creep away, feeling dirty.

"It's a disaster!" Zinta meets me outside the entrance to the dining hall. Her face is screwed up into a knot of worry. She pounds one fist into the palm of her other hand.

Sounds like a baseball hitting a catcher's mitt. *Pow pow pow.*

"Huh?"

"I had a flush! A flush, for heaven's sake. All diamonds! How did I know he'd have four of a kind? The big fat ape. Get in there, Alan. They're waiting!"

She pushes me hard enough to knock me over, almost.

"Huh?" I say.

Eric and Derek are inside. They look mad. I wonder who they're mad at?

"It's your fault," says Eric.

Oh. I guess they're mad at me.

"I did what you told me," he says. "There were two of us left: me and this pimply Trailblazer kid they call the Calculator. And I bet without looking at my hand."

"I never told you to bet –"

"And he called me. And he had a good hand. And I didn't. It's your fault!"

They all lost. The poker final is me against three Trailblazers. I represent the sole Lumberjack hope for the games. I am Zinta's chance to hang on to the Master Tripper Scroll. Great.

"Did Trixie win?" I ask.

Derek nods his head. "I thought I had her at the end," he says. "I drew two cards and ended up with two pair. She drew three cards, and ended up with three of a kind. You'd better watch her, Alan. She's good."

"The Calculator is good too," says Eric. "He's really smart. He knows all the odds for everything."

Campers are still calling out, and laughing, and eating and drinking, and moving around. Fewer and fewer are playing. I guess they're running out of chips. The roulette wheel spins slowly, slowly. *Clack* . . . *clack* .... *clack.* Sounds like a bag of popcorn in the microwave.

The microphone booms out: "ALAN DINGWALL, COME TO THE POKER TABLE. THE FINAL IS ABOUT TO START." Funny to hear your name bouncing around the rafters.

I'm still trying to believe what I saw earlier. Christopher and the nurse! The thought makes me all creepy inside. I am not in any condition to play poker.

"Huh?" I say. Zinta is talking to me. "What was that?"

"Weren't you listening?"

"Come on up, Alan!" Boomer is standing on a chair. She waves me forward. Campers turn to stare at me. Those with the green LUMBERJACK shirts are smiling and clapping. Those in the yellow TRAILBLAZER shirts are staring coldly. There's Victor! He smiles nervously at me, then looks away. Thanks, Victor.

The referee for the final is a redheaded girl with a ring in her nose. The ring is gold, to match her TRAILBLAZER shirt.

"Hi, Alan," says Trixie. She introduces me around the table, as polite as pie, as if she's never punched me in the nose. Very strange. Like we're guests at a garden party. Behind me I can feel Zinta breathing heavily. A small pimply guy on my right says hello. He'll be the Calculator. The fourth guy at the table is a lummox with long dark hair and a gold tooth. "Hey – oh!" he says, and belches loudly. He may be the only person in camp not wearing a team T-shirt. His is a vivid Hawaiian number, with a missing button.

"Quiet, Dudley!" says Trixie.

He belches again, and smiles at me. His gold tooth winks.

I wonder where Dudley has been all day. I'm sure I'd have noticed him.

I say hello. There's only one empty chair at the table. I take it, and look around. Come on, Dingwall. Pay attention. There's nothing you can do about Christopher and the nurse. This is something you can do. Play cards. I try to get my head back in the game.

I think I like my spot. I'm behind the Calculator. He'll probably be cautious. Dudley looks like a wild and crazy guy. I'd rather be in front of him. Trixie is right opposite me. I take out my stack of forty chips.

The counselor with the ring in her nose speaks up. "We'll still be playing draw poker, no wild cards. Pot limit. Three raises." She doesn't explain the rules. This is the final. We know the rules.

Trixie is shuffling the deck. I find myself thinking about the scene in the storage shed. Do I really feel . . .

– *Did you come here to sit around or to play cards!* shouts Norbert. *Deal!*

Calculator stares at me and doesn't say anything. Dudley chuckles. Trixie drops the deck so that it spills all over the table. Dudley laughs loudly. Trixie glares at me.

The first few hands pass in a daze. I don't see any really good cards. I don't bet. I'm still processing the information. Christopher and the nurse. What does it mean to me? To Mom? I don't like him kissing her, but I don't like him kissing anyone else when he should be with her. Do I tell her? Do I tell anyone? I wish I could stop the world for a bit, and take some time to pull myself together.

Calculator deals. I pick up my cards automatically. All black. Like my thoughts. I put the hand facedown on the table.

Everyone looks at me. Must be my turn to bet. "Check," I say.

"Five!" That's Dudley. He has a glutton's approach to poker: more is better. He shovels poker chips into the pot the way Victor shovels potato chips into his mouth.

"Your five, and five more," says Trixie. Her lips are thin with strain.

Calculator is taking his time. He blinks rapidly, checking his hand once more.

"All right. Ten chips to me. I'm in."

Silence. "Hey, Alan," says Dudley. He's fingering his pile of chips.

"Huh?" Oh, no! I've forgotten my cards. I pick up the hand.

– *We're in*, says Norbert. *Your ten and ten more!*

I don't move. What has Norbert done to me? That's half my stack of chips!

"Come on, Alan," says the counselor. "Put the chips in."

"But I . . . I didn't. . . ."

They're all staring at me. I don't know how to explain about Norbert. I find myself pushing twenty chips into the middle.

"Oh, boy," I mutter. Just what I need right now is Norbert feeling feisty.

– *Let's play poker! That's fifteen to you, big guy!*

Dudley stares at me. "You didn't bet right away, and now you're raising the bet," he says. "Check and raise? Smells fishy. I don't like it. I'm out."

That's the first time he hasn't bet.

I lean back in my chair. "Where did you learn to play cards, Norbert?" I whisper.

– *We have poker on Jupiter. Everyone learns at school. Poker and hopscotch.*

"Quiet," says Trixie. "I'm trying to think."

– *In or out isn't too hard, girlie. Flip a coin.*

"Hey," says the counselor.

"Sorry," I say.

Trixie pushes a pile of chips into the middle.

– *Should be ten chips there*, says Norbert.

"Why, you little. . . . There *are* ten chips."

She spreads them out to show. There are ten. Calculator hesitates, then he counts out his chips too. Three of us are in so far. Now the all-important draw.

"How many cards?" Calculator asks me.

I still haven't checked my hand. Before I can look, Norbert answers.

– No cards.

Calculator pauses a second. Dudley's out, so it's Trixie's turn next. She glares at me, keeps three cards and takes two. Can she have three of a kind? Maybe. Probably.

Calculator himself takes three cards. He must be holding a pair of aces. Nothing else would be worth twenty chips to him.

A ring of people is forming around the table, watching the game. No one says much, but the attention is a bit disturbing. "Keep back, please," calls the counselor. "Give the players room."

My bet first. I still don't know what I have.

– Might as well bet ten more, says Norbert. *Either you can beat a flush or you can't.*

I'm glad I'm not looking at my hand because I might have missed Trixie's eyes widen when Norbert says the word "flush." She can't beat it. Three of a kind is a good hand, but a flush is better.

Well, well.

Dudley is staring at me and shaking his head. "You trying to make us mad?" he says. "Talking all the time?"

"No," I say.

– Yes, says Norbert.

"Which is it?'

– Angry people have bad judgment. They think about punching someone in the nose, when the best thing to do would

be to smile and fold their cards. Isn't that true, Trixie?

She's staring at me. Her left hand is clenched into a fist. Her clean, tanned knuckles stand out like pecans. Her jaw works.

"Very . . . funny," she says. "I'm not mad. I don't need to chase the pot. I can act rationally. I . . . fold."

Calculator folds too. Well, well, well! I've won a good pot without showing my cards. I have more chips than anyone else. Zinta is standing off to one side. She claps her hands loudly, and calls, "Come on, Lumberjacks!" Trixie shoots her a glance of pure hatred, and grabs my cards.

"Let's see this flush, this . . . what?" She stares. "WHAT IS THIS? I can't BELIEVE it! You were BLUFFING!!" She throws the cards onto the table for everyone to see.

"Was I?" I say.

– *No,* says Norbert.

But the cards don't lie. There they are, four clubs and a spade. All black, like I remember. But not a flush. I guess I was bluffing, after all.

– *Pretty good, eh?* says Norbert. *Ace high.*

"Um . . . that's not a flush," I whisper.

– *They're all the same color. On Jupiter, that's a good hand.*

"Well, here, a flush is all the same suit."

– *Suit? What do you mean, "suit"? Like all plaid? All pinstripes? That's a flush?*

"Forget it, Norbert."

Dudley shakes his head. Zinta laughs. Trixie is so mad she picks up my cards again, and rips them in half. We have to get a new deck.

25

Fours

My favorite book about cards offers this piece of wisdom. There is, says the book, a sucker at every card table. Look around the table. If you can't spot the sucker, get up and go. It's you.

I expect Trixie to go ballistic now – to make a run at me every chance she gets. But ripping my cards seems to have calmed her down. The counselor finds another deck. Trixie plays quietly, with concentration. She seems to be biding her time. Dudley keeps betting. You might think it's hard to tell what he's got, since he bets high with a bad hand *and* with a good one, but in fact he's easy to read. When he's bluffing, he puts his cards down on the table with a slap. When he has a good hand, he lays it down more carefully. My card book calls this a *tell*. The action *tells* me what he has.

Trixie's deal. As usual I watch the other players as they pick up their hands. Calculator's eyes widen slightly. May be a good hand. Dudley chuckles to himself. Trixie looks blank.

I check my cards quickly. A good hand, for once. Trip fours. Three of a kind, even three fours, is good enough to win most pots. And who knows – I might improve when I draw.

Calculator bets four chips. I call his bet. I have a good enough hand to raise, but there's no point in advertising yet. Dudley slaps down his cards. "Well, well! See your four, and raise five," he says.

Across the table from me, Trixie folds. Calculator stays, and so do I. He draws one card. Must have started with two pair. Probably high pairs. I hem and haw, and then draw two cards. The hemming and hawing are to make Dudley think I don't like my hand. He makes a big deal about drawing only one card, then slaps the hand down on the table. I pick up my two cards. I'm hoping to pick up a pair. With my three fours that would give me a full house – a really really good hand. Mind you, three of a kind will beat Dudley's bluff and Calculator's two pair.

Final round of betting. Calculator slides out two chips. I decide to call instead of raising. This might backfire. If Dudley backs down, I won't have won much. But I have confidence in Dudley. And he doesn't let me down. He yawns, stretching his arms over his head. His Hawaiian shirt rides up over his round brown belly. He scratches himself. He seems to fill the table. "Time to get the kids off the streets," he says, and bets the pot limit.

It's a big bet. Thirty-one chips. Dudley's only got a couple left. He might as well quit if he doesn't win. He pulls down his shirt.

Calculator stares past me. He's thinking. I can almost hear the wheels turning in his mind. "You're bluffing, Dudley," he says.

Dudley laughs. He doesn't look nervous.

"I call," says Calculator. He counts the chips carefully.

I feel, rather than see, Dudley sag. Yup, his "tell" gave him away. He was bluffing. If I had any doubt before, I don't now.

Calculator notices the sag too. He looks pleased with himself.

My bet. Time to step in. "I'll see the thirty-one, and raise twenty more."

Trixie groans. Calculator gasps. He's forgotten about me.

Dudley throws in his hand. "I'm done," he says with a laugh. "I quit. I'll take a couple of turns at roulette."

Calculator is staring at me. I wink at him.

– *Is this as good a hand as the pinstripe suit?* asks Norbert. *On Jupiter, fours are not good cards.*

"*Shhh,*" I say.

Dudley gets to his feet. "I been meaning to tell you, Alan. That squeaky voice of yours is really –"

"Distracting?" I answer for him. "I know. I'm sorry. It's kind of a long story."

"I was going to say 'weird,'" says Dudley. "See you!" He lumbers away from the table.

Calculator is talking to Trixie. "Come on!" she says. "You can't fold."

"I don't think he's bluffing."

"Didn't you hear about the pinstripe suit? Remember the flush? He's bluffing. He fooled Dudley."

"Yes, but twenty chips is all I have left. I'll be out."

"You'll win. You'll be fine. He's got nothing! He's worthless!"

She's staring at me.

– *Boy, the number of times Nerissa has said that to me*, says Norbert. *I feel like I'm back home on Jupiter. Mind you, Nerissa doesn't look like a horse.*

Trixie chokes. "A horse!"

"*Shhh*, Norbert."

"Are you saying I look like a horse?"

"No," I say.

She grabs the Calculator by his TRAILBLAZER T-shirt, and pulls him towards her. "I'll lend you some chips," she says.

"Hey!" I say in a loud voice. "Can she do that? Can she lend him chips?"

The crowd around our table is bigger than I remember. They're all paying attention. I turn around to look for Zinta. She's got her back to me, talking to some other Lumberjacks. I notice the rose tattoo on the back of her leg.

The referee nods. "I don't see why not."

"But then it's like I'm playing against both of them."

"Well, you are," she says. "You're a Lumberjack, and they're Trailblazers."

"Oh, yeah," I say.

Trixie and Calculator are talking in low voices. "Do it," she says.

The entire dining hall has gone quiet. No one is playing skee ball or roulette. The circle around us has grown. And it has moved closer. And the expressions on people's faces have got uglier. Green shirts are jostling against yellow shirts. Owls against Skunks, Chipmunks against Weasels, Hummingbirds against Foxes. I feel like I'm part of some primitive food chain.

Calculator swallows. "See your twenty," he says, "and raise . . . a hundred."

"What?" I say.

Trixie is reaching behind her, into the crowd, grabbing handfuls of chips and pushing them across the table. Calculator is counting them. Stack after stack. The table is filling up.

"Three raise limit," calls the referee. "That's the last raise. Alan, you must fold or call."

"But . . . I haven't got a hundred chips."

Referee says nothing.

One hand can change the whole game, says my card book. Luck, skill, power – they all flow together towards the winner. One hand can change that flow for the whole game. And it looks like this is the one hand. I look across the table. I can't see Trixie or the Calculator as a sucker. Does that mean I should get up and go?

"Yes, you do." Zinta's voice in my ear.

"What?"

"You do have a hundred chips."

Zinta's hand on my shoulder. I feel her fingers digging in. *Ouch.* "I've been collecting from the Lumberjacks here. There's over a hundred chips in this bag." She holds out a plastic bag, solemnly, formally, like it's some sort of sacred trust. I am the hope for the Lumberjacks. I take the bag, as seriously as I can. Actually, I'm trying to resist an urge to laugh. This is casino night at a summer camp in Ontario. We're not talking about the fate of the galaxy here. *Luke, I am your father* sounds okay. *Luke, I am your baby-sitter* doesn't have the same ring to it. *Oh, and Luke, you're not supposed to play video games until you take out the garbage.*

"Well, well – how's it all going?" Boomer elbows her way to the front of the circle. Gosh, she takes up a lot of room. "Getting late, you know. After nine o'clock. You younger campers will have to be getting back to your cabins."

Muted rustling from the circle of green and yellow.

Boomer's eyebrows go up as she looks at the table. "So, this is the big hand, hey? Are the team captains here? Oh, there you are, Trixie, I didn't see you behind all the poker chips! And Zinta. Good. Seems like this year's games day depends on Alan and Oliver."

I weigh the bag of chips in my hand. Calculator – it's impossible to think of him as Oliver – says nothing. Boomer waddles away. "I'll be in the kitchen if anyone wants me," she says over her shoulder.

Trixie's on her feet, glaring across the table at Zinta. And Zinta is glaring right back.

"You can't buy the hand, Trixie, the way you buy everything else." Zinta crashes her fist onto the table. The stacks of chips quiver.

"Careful, dear!" says Trixie. "You know how violent you can be!"

The growling goes around the circle ring. There are a few counselors around. They seem uncomfortable. "Um, let's go," says the referee. "Alan, do you want to bet or fold?"

– *On Jupiter,* says Norbert, *I'd fold this hand like linguine!*

"Huh?"

– *Do I mean linguine? You know what I mean.*

"No, I don't." I don't have to look at my hand again. I slide the bag of chips into the center of the table.

"Call," I say.

Silence.

– *Origami,* says Norbert. *That's the word. Linguine is something else.*

So what does he have? The room is silent as Calculator turns over his cards one at a time. "Three jacks . . . ," he says. There's an exhalation from the crowd. ". . . *and two tens.*" His fingers are trembling.

There's his full house! A good hand. A really good hand. Wow. His jacks are worth more than my fours.

The crowd surges forward.

"Ha-ha!" crows Trixie. Her jaw stretches out when she laughs. It elongates her face, making her look even more, well, horsey.

"Can you beat it?" Zinta demands. "Can you beat the full house, Alan? Can you?"

Again, silence. Christopher and the nurse are part of the crowd. I look away. I can't deal with that now. Eric and Derek are standing side by side, frowning anxiously, fists raised to shoulder level, willing me to win.

I'm surprised to see that my hand is shaking too. This really matters to me. I take a deep breath to calm myself, and smile up at Trixie. It's Calculator's hand, but it's Trixie I want to beat. She's the one who punched me. "I have two pair –" I begin.

"What?" interrupts Zinta from behind me. "Were you bluffing?"

Trixie's face puckers. "Two pair? Ha!"

"– of fours," I finish.

"Two pair of . . ." They're working it out. I turn over my hand. Four fours. And a queen, but who cares? Four fours is great. I was hoping for a full house, but I did even better.

The crowd reacts like a big wave hitting the pier, leaping high, their shouts raining down on us. "Lumberjacks win!" cries Zinta, shaking me back and forth from behind. "We win! Way to go, Alan!"

Calculator sags forward onto the table. Trixie turns white beneath her tan. She gasps for breath. "Ahh!" she cries, shaking her long head back and forth, blowing out with her lips like a motor boat. No, not a motor boat. More like a . . .

– *Whoa, Misty!* Norbert makes a very convincing whinnying noise.

Yeah, that's it. More like a horse.

"You!" says Trixie.

– *Long mane and horseshoes, we win and YOU LOSE!*

Trixie lunges forward and grabs me by the throat.

– *Oh, no, you don't!* shouts Norbert. *You are going DOWN! Come on, Lumberjacks!!*

I hear a confused roaring from all over. Without using my hands, I break Trixie's hold on my throat. My head snaps up towards her as if it's spring-loaded. I drift between sleeping and waking, this world and some other one.

I'm back in the garage, at the space shuttle launch, staring at the mirrored helmet of the second astronaut. I lift my left eyebrow and so does my reflection. But that's wrong. In the mirror I'd be lifting my right eyebrow. I take a clumsy step back. And I realize the second astronaut is me. I'm watching myself board a spaceship. So who's the other astronaut in the garage – the one hopping ahead of me? I take another clumsy step. The space suit is so awkward.

The other astronaut turns around.

– Remember I said that one of these days I might ask you for help? says a familiar voice.

26

Norbert Nose

Is Coming Home!

It takes Boomer and the counselors more than half an hour to clear up the riot in the dining hall. That's what Boomer calls it: a riot. She's angry. No one's seriously hurt, but there are an incredible number of contusions, abrasions, bruises, cuts, and scrapes. Dr. Callous and the nurse are run off their feet, patching and wrapping, poking and stitching well into the night. The infirmary looks like a small-scale version of that scene in *Gone with the Wind*, with the wounded spread out in all directions.

Did I say there were no serious injuries? Well, none except Christopher's. His ankle was crushed in the rumpus. He has to go to the hospital in Peterborough for X rays and maybe to have a pin put in.

One by one the campers leave the infirmary to go back to their cabins. Boomer stands grimly in the doorway. "I hope you're sorry for the way you behaved!" she says, as the yellow and green shirts leave. Or, "You deserve your sprained wrist!" or, more often, "I'm surprised at you!" No one has a comeback. Boomer is right, and they all know it.

The campers come over to say good-bye to me and Victor, when they find out we'll be leaving tonight. Boomer made the phone call to Cobourg. "I told your mom she could come and pick you up tomorrow, but she wanted to come right now."

"My mom said that?" I ask. Doesn't sound like her.

"I was talking to Mrs. Grunewald. She misses you, Victor."

He rolls his eyes.

"You guys should come to camp here next summer," says one of the Trailblazers. There's blood on his T-shirt, and his hand is bandaged. "This was the best games day ever!"

The Owls and Beavers shake my hand on the way out. "Thanks, Alan," says Eric. "You won the games for us. You are one heckuva player."

No one has ever said that to me before.

The doctor spends more time on Trixie than anyone else. She is one of the last to go. The counselors found her on the floor of the dining hall, underneath a pile of bodies, with her hands over her face. Now her nose is packed with cotton, and she breathes through her open mouth. She comes out of the treatment room and marches up to Boomer.

"You wait until I tell my daddy –" she starts.

"Be quiet!" The CAMP DIRECTOR button on Boomer's hat jiggles in indignation. "I spoke to your father already, Trixie. He's as disappointed in you as I am. I still can't understand how you – a senior girl, a camp leader – could have started this riot."

"It wasn't me!" screams Trixie. With her packed nose, it sounds like she has a cold. *Id wazid be!* I look away, so I won't laugh. "It wasn't my fault. It was the new guy – Alan. *He* started it."

"What do you mean, Trixie? Everyone says you grabbed him first. And Zinta was –"

"Zinta? ZINTA?" Of course it comes out *ZID-DA?* Trixie is mad enough to spit nickels.

Zinta is sitting with me and Victor. Trixie glares at her. "Just wait til next year, you trash!" she says.

Dext year.

"Go to your cabin, Trixie," says Boomer. "Don't threaten anyone. I doubt we'll even have a games day next year!"

Trixie goes out, slamming the door.

Zinta's unhurt, except for a scrape on her arm, from pulling me out of a pileup of bodies. She crosses the room, puts her hand on the camp director's shoulder. "I'm sorry, Boomer," she says. "I'm glad Alan beat Trixie at cards, and I'm glad we won the games. But I didn't want any of the rest of this."

"I know, dear," says Boomer.

Zinta thanks us both again. "I'll never travel without a safety pin, Victor," she tells him. He blushes and looks away. "And I'll never forget that last hand, Alan. What a player!" She takes something out of her pocket and flattens it on the table. "Would you . . . sign my Master Tripper Scroll?" she asks.

What can I say? "Sure." I sign. She shakes my hand. I stare up into her face.

"Hey, your eyes are brown!" I say. "Dark brown, like maple syrup. I never noticed anyone else's eyes before."

She smiles uneasily, and releases my hand.

The ambulance arrives for Christopher. It's a two hour trip to Peterborough. I wonder how bumpy it will be. The night is warm and dark. I can see lots of bugs in the infirmary floodlights. The moon is yellow, and almost full. I can't tell if it's waxing or waning.

Before Christopher goes, there's something I have to tell him. I march over. He's sitting up on his padded stretcher on wheels. His eyes are level with mine.

"I know what's on your mind," he says.

"Do you?"

"It's about your mom, isn't it? We had a long talk last night. She's okay with it, I think. She understands how much Bernice means to me. She's a wonderful person, don't you think?"

My head is whirling. "Who?"

"Bernice, of course."

The nurse is fussing over Christopher, helping the ambulance guys strap him onto the stretcher. She stands up now, flushed and sweaty and tired. There are dark stains on her uniform. She's had a busy night.

"Hi," she says, with a shy smile.

Christopher puts his arm around her waist. She doesn't fight him off. "We're going to get married," he says.

I don't know what to do. Shake hands, I guess, and congratulate him. She looks happy. So does he, though I notice that his eyes are still straying around the room.

"I thought you were living with Mrs. Dingwall," says Victor, with a frown. That's Victor, always saying what he means. Bernice's face darkens a shade.

"What's this, Christopher?" she says.

The ambulance guys pick up the stretcher and slide it into the back of the ambulance.

"No, no, Vic. Not *living* with her. Sure, I used to spend time with her. But I've explained all that to Bernice."

"Christopher?" she says again.

The doors close from the inside. Victor leads me away.

"Hey!" Bernice pounds on the outside of the ambulance. "Hey!! Christopher Leech, answer me!"

The ambulance drives off.

Mrs. Grunewald is early. She sniffs, and wipes her eyes, and hugs us both for a long time.

I sit back in my seat and look out the window of the minivan. The telephone poles fly past. The moon hangs in front of the van like a Ritz cracker with a bite out of it. Mrs. Grunewald doesn't say anything about Camp Omega. She doesn't ask about Christopher. How much does she know?

She digs into a small picnic hamper. "You boys must be hungry," she says. "D'you fancy one of these, now? They're advertised on the television. Supposed to be that good for you."

She's holding out two health bars, in their familiar gold wrappers. We both decline.

"Your ma wanted to come up with me, Alan," she says. "But she's busy throwing his things away. There're clothes all over your front lawn."

"Christopher – Leech's clothes?"

"Aye. And papers and other things too."

I think back to our conversation a few days ago, when my mom accused me of not accepting the olive branch of friendship. Here she is, scattering personal stuff like breadcrumbs.

I think of my house with no trace of Christopher. I think of him and Bernice the nurse. I can't help it. I start to smile. I settle back against the cushioned seat, and smile and smile, while the night zooms past and the broken lines on the highway lead all the way to the moon.

I'm in the spaceship now, in my clumsy suit. I hear Norbert's voice again. He's singing one of Christopher's army marching songs. Only with new words.

– Milky Way is shining bright.
Jupiter is on the right.
Cocoa's in your special cup.
Come on, Dingwall, buckle up!
Honey, disconnect the phone.
Norbert Nose is coming home.

What on earth? I can feel my stomach heaving, the way it does on a roller coaster. Skin on my face is pulling away. We're moving really fast. The front window is huge, and rounded. The stars look so bright, so close. I feel I can touch them. Then they disappear into a blur of light. Next thing I know, we're approaching a giant planet ringed in cloud.

– If my mother asks you, remember to tell her I've been wearing my bed socks.

No. Wait. I'm ahead of myself again.

Information about other Norbert books by Richard Scrimger:

The Nose from Jupiter
(the first book in the series)

Alan isn't brave or strong, and he's not much good at soccer.
What's more, he seems to be a bully magnet. Everything changes
one day when Norbert, a tiny alien from Jupiter, takes up residence
in Alan's nose. Alan's condition baffles medical science, but it
gives him a whole new and hilarious way to solve his problems.

Winner of the Mr. Christie's Book Award
Kid's Pick of the Lists – American Booksellers Association

A Nose for Adventure
(the second book in the series)

Alan is off to New York to meet his father for some "quality" time.
There are some snags, though. First, his father isn't at the airport;
and then he's kidnapped, with his seatmate Frieda. Sally, an aban-
doned mutt, joins the scene, and then, finally, Norbert returns.
Alan had been an unwilling host to Norbert, but when you're lost
in New York City, being chased by bad guys, you need all the help
you can get! *A Nose for Adventure* is another wild ride on Richard
Scrimger's hilarious, rollercoaster of a novel.

The Nose from Jupiter   ISBN 0-88776-428-2
A Nose for Adventure   ISBN 0-88776-499-1